se for
Beverley Naidoo's
CHAIN OF FIRE

"Beverley Naidoo was detained briefly in the 1960s in the crackdown against opponents of apartheid. Nelson Mandela and other ANC leaders went to prison for life. In exile Mrs Naidoo has become a prize-winning children's novelist. Her first children's book *Journey to Jo'burg*, sold 30,000 copies in this country. Mrs Naidoo's second book, *Chain of Fire*, is a sequel for older children. The descriptions of forced removal come from the testimonies of hundreds of the four million people uprooted so far. They are driven out and into limbo as part of the South African government's strategy to ensure the survival of apartheid."

– Victoria Brittain, *Guardian*

"This extraordinarily powerful and gripping novel should be compulsory reading in South Africa's white high schools. It won't be." –*Johannesburg Weekly Mail*

"Beverley Naidoo's *Chain of Fire* is living history, its details, shaped into fiction, need no heightening. A valuable book, a compelling read." – *Observer*

"Do not be surprised if young people who read this moving account of man's inhumanity to man, take part in protest marches outside South Africa House. It has the capacity to stir the emotions and remain in the memory long after other stories have been read and forgotten." –*Junior Bookshelf*

"The series of events which the villagers have to endure are described with economy but poignance, allowing the horror of the events to speak for itself. I wish that this book could be prescribed reading in every white South African secondary school."

– *Dragon's Teeth*

"From first to last we see things from the black perspective. The villagers are not by choice 'activists'. They are people at home, attached to a long established way of life which differs from its white equivalents only in the terrible impoverishment of permitted standards. This powerful indictment of the 'homeland' policy will help young readers to penetrate beyond political argument to human realities."

– *Times Educational Supplement*

Chain of Fire

Beverley Naidoo

Lions

Other titles in Lions and Tracks about South Africa:

Journey to Jo'burg *Beverley Naidoo*
Go Well, Stay Well *Toeckey Jones*
Waiting for the Rain *Sheila Gordon*
Somehow Tenderness Survives *Hazel Rochman*

First published in Great Britain 1989 by Collins
Published in Lions in 1990
Second impression November 1990

Lions is an imprint of
the Children's Division, part of
HarperCollins Publishers Ltd,
8 Grafton Street, London W1X 3LA

Printed and bound in Great Britain by
William Collins Sons & Co. Ltd, Glasgow

Three and a half million people have been removed. A further 1,934,650 are under threat. . .

Surplus People's Project,
South Africa, 1985

"We formed a group and asked the police the cause but the answer was to be pointed with guns."

Former resident of
Tsitsikama Forest, Cape

Chain of Fire is dedicated to all those who have struggled to resist.

CHAPTER 1

"Come over here, Ausi Naledi! Look here!"

Tiro stared at the number 1427 scrawled boldly in fresh white paint across the door of their house. He was on his way out to the village tap to collect the morning's water. Drips of paint were still settling down cracks in the old wood. Lightly he touched the '4' and white paint stuck to his finger. His nose wrinkled with suspicion as he turned to Naledi, his fifteen-year-old sister. Even in the dimness of the house, fear showed in her dark eyes.

"Who did it Ausi Naledi? We didn't hear anything!"

Naledi shook her head, silent.

Wriggling between them, their little sister Dineo stretched and jumped to the full height of her four years, trying to touch the paint.

"No Dineo! It's still wet!"

Pulling the child gently away from the door, Naledi held her small hand as they ran out to the low mud wall surrounding their yard.

"That's the one!"

Tiro's eyes shifted up the dusty track of the village

road. In the distance, coming into view from behind a house with a tin roof, was a man in yellow overalls carrying a tin and brush. A group of people was gathering. The man seemed to be backing away. Still holding Dineo's hand, Naledi began to jog up the track. Tiro, eleven years old and agile, soon sprinted ahead. With thin, strong legs below frayed khaki shorts he ran effortlessly. Large white numbers glared out from the doors of the other houses they passed. As they got closer, they could hear their neighbour Mma Tshadi's voice rising above the rest. Her large arms seemed to be sweeping the man backwards.

"Don't you touch my house! Don't you step on my path!"

"Intshwarele Mma . . . excuse me . . . It's not my wish. It's the government's wish. The government 'baas' says I must put the numbers on all the houses here."

He pulled out some paper from his pocket, but quickly stuffed it back as Mma Tshadi thrust out her hand to take it. At that moment the sound of an engine caused everyone to turn. A blue car edged slowly forward from behind the small thatched and stone church building further up the road. Two white men, both in pale-coloured suits and ties, climbed out.

"What's the trouble then?" asked one of them with a brief-case under his arm. He spoke in English.

"This lady . . . she doesn't want me to put the number on her door, baas."

The man in yellow overalls seemed to stand a little taller, now that his 'boss' was with him. He even spoke in English now, not in Tswana. Slowly surveying the group, the man opened his brief-case and pulled out some papers.

"Don't you people know you have to move from here? The trucks are already booked to come for you in four weeks' time now. So that's why you must have numbers on your houses. Then the whole thing can be done in a proper, orderly way and there won't be any upsets."

There was a stunned hush. Mma Tshadi was the first to speak.

"What do you mean 'move from here'? These are our homes. We live here. What do you mean 'trucks are coming'?"

Naledi's heart beat fast. This white man must be from 'Affairs', from the Government, but Mma Tshadi wasn't frightened to talk up to him, speaking his language with a heavy Tswana accent. Younger than their grandmother Nono, she was a large woman with thick square shoulders and with a voice which had always been loud. The man from 'Affairs' looked directly at Mma Tshadi.

"Do you pay rent to Chief Sekete?"

Mma Tshadi nodded very slightly. Underneath the floral scarf tied at the back her face was taut, sharply chiselled like stone.

"So you're a tenant . . . Well, if you don't know about the move that's not our fault. The landowners here, Chief Sekete and his family, were informed long ago and we've had no complaints. In fact your chief has seen the place where you're going. I even heard him say that it's better than here. So you must ask him, not us. Now, let my boy get on with his job painting up the numbers."

He raised his narrow eyebrows as he looked over at the man with the paint.

"Hurry up, John. We haven't got all day."

Quiet with shock, the group stood watching as the man in yellow overalls hurried up the path to Mma Tshadi's house and, first checking with the paper in his pocket, slapped a number across the door . . . 1438. Then he made his way across to the next house . . . 1439 . . . and the next. Saying nothing, but looking grim and determined, Mma Tshadi set off, followed by others, in the direction of Chief Sekete's house.

CHAPTER 2

"What does he mean . . . trucks are coming for us in four weeks' time? To go where?" Tiro's eyes were anxious, his voice angry. "Let's go with Mma Tshadi to find out."

He pulled at Naledi's elbow but she held back. She was thinking of their grandmother in whose house they all lived.

"No. I must tell Nono first. You go with them."

As Tiro hurried after the others, Naledi glanced at the two white men standing by the car. They watched her and glanced round at the village. Its houses, most of them mud-walled with thatch or corrugated iron roofs, sprawled uncluttered along earthen paths and stretches of dry grass from its low western slope down to flat veld – grazing land interspersed with fields. The white men seemed so sure of themselves in their smart suits and with the power of their pieces of paper. What right did they have to come like this, threatening to plough up a whole village? Naledi's grip on her sister's hand tightened as she set off across the stubbly grass in the opposite direction to Tiro.

It was a long walk to the white-owned farm where Nono worked. At first Dineo trotted alongside, but when she became tired Naledi swung her up onto her back.

"Ausi Naledi, Nono must tell the man to make the door clean," Dineo insisted to her big sister, pushing her hands a little too roughly into the pockets of her faded orange skirt so that a finger tore through the thin cotton. Biting her lip, she looked up guiltily. But Naledi walked on, without reply or comment. Her little sister hadn't understood the conversation in English between the white man and Mma Tshadi and thought that Nono could put everything right.

They followed the route which Nono had taken early that morning. First they passed the field where the mielie stalks, looking grey and parched, had managed to push their way through hard clods of earth. Beyond these, a few rows of cabbages and straggling pumpkin leaves were still trying to survive. They walked across the rough veld, where villagers let their cattle graze, and then up to the road between the wire fences of the farms owned by white people. Once here, the earth looked softer and leaves were varying shades of real green. Metal pipes carrying water ran alongside rows of fresh healthy plants. You could already see the young cobs of mielies beginning to fatten beneath the silky tassles. But today Naledi hardly noticed them.

So many thoughts were racing through her mind. How could Chief Sekete have reached an agreement with these white people? When he had first heard of the plans for removal, why hadn't he spoken of them at the kgotla, the place where all village matters were discussed? This land had belonged to the Sekete family for over seventy years, from before the time when the law said only whites could buy land. Everyone knew the story how Chief Sekete's grandfather had bought this farm from an Englishman who had decided that farming here wasn't for him and complained that the rain was too unreliable, not like in the land far across the sea from where he had come. There it rained every year without fail. The story had been passed on along with the name of their village. Almost certainly as a comment on the Englishman, Chief Sekete's grandfather had called this place Bophelong, 'the place where we get life'. They would survive, like their ancestors before them, the hardships of a land where water was scarce. The Deed of Transfer for Bophelong was proudly framed on the equally old wooden sideboard in Chief Sekete's house. It began with the phrase, 'Know All Men Whom It May Concern . . .' Naledi knew those fancily curved English words off by heart. The chief's daughter Poleng was her closest friend, and Naledi was a frequent visitor to the house. The chief had always seemed especially kind to her as her own father was dead. But what could she think now? Was it possible that Poleng too had known about the removal and had not said anything? The thought repelled her.

The news she carried would be a terrible shock to their grandmother, which was why Naledi wanted to tell her herself. Nono looked after them while their mother worked far off in the city for a white family. The law would not let Mma keep her children with her. And how would Mma take the news? She was so far away, what could she do? Naledi's mind went back to the time once before when there had been a grave threat to the family. When she was a baby, Dineo had become dangerously ill, so ill that Naledi and Tiro had made the long journey to Jo'burg all by themselves to fetch their mother. They had been fortunate. Dineo had recovered, but the doctor had said she must have milk, fruit and vegetables or she would become ill again. Where they lived such food was scarce and expensive and Mma had to pay off the money she had borrowed for the train fares and hospital. So on Saturdays, both Naledi and Tiro had often walked, just after sunrise, all the way to the white people's town to earn money. They would wait outside the supermarket, offering to push the trolleys laden with groceries or carry the boxes and bags of white shoppers. It was a gamble. Sometimes they would not be paid anything, sometimes just one or two cents. Along with other children waiting to earn left-over coins, they kept a careful eye out for police, ready to dart away at the first sign of a uniform.

Nono hadn't wanted the children to do this work, but had been forced to agree that whatever money they earned was necessary. Like most of the older people around, Nono herself had not been able to find any paid work. She was no longer as strong as she used to be. Then, by chance, a friend who had worked in the garden at white farm became too ill to continue and she had sent Nono in her place. At first the white woman at the farmhouse had said Nono looked too old, but as the work was mainly weeding she would try her out.

"I have to be careful whom I have near the house these days. I suppose I can trust someone older like you," she had added.

The pay was only R5 each week. On rare occasions Nono was given a few oranges or vegetables when the farm produced more than was needed. But Nono would always stop at the farm's dairy and exchange a few precious cents for a little can filled with milk for Dineo. Yes, money had always been a great struggle for the family, but somehow they were managing with their various small incomes. They were even saving to buy a goat, so Nono would not have to buy milk. Why did this new threat have to come to them now? In her heart, Naledi knew that was a foolish question. Dreadful things were happening to other people all the time. She had learnt so much through her friendship with Grace Mbatha, the young woman from Soweto who had helped her and Tiro when they had been looking for their mother in Jo'burg when Dineo was sick. Ever since then they had been writing to each other. There were always threats where Grace lived in Soweto, near Jo'burg, and recently Naledi had begun to worry that her friend might be in trouble herself. As she had not heard from her for some time, Naledi had written again, but there had still been no reply. Grace's letters often carried news of protests against schools, rents, taxes, of stonings, burnings, of attacks by police, shootings and arrests. Even army troops had come into Soweto in massive tanks. Grace wrote about these things in a sort of code:

"Have you ever seen hippos in your river? They are terrible in a rage, but if you are angry enough you forget to be scared."

Grace knew perfectly well that there was no flowing river near Bophelong any more, only a dry river bed. 'Hippos' were army tanks. Often the news in the letters matched up with bits of information passed on from someone visiting the city or from a fleeting item on the radio.

> 'Police in Soweto report three people dead in continuing violence yesterday. The Prime Minister, Mr P.W. Botha, has said that his government would not be forced from its present path. Speaking in Parliament today, Mr Botha said he would not shirk from taking whatever measures were necessary . . .'

Reading Grace's letters usually left Naledi feeling angry and upset. She found it difficult to express her outrage. Here in Bophelong she was so far away and quite unable to help. Yet now, all of a sudden, they too were thrust into danger . . . and she was unprepared. Her stomach wound in a tight knot.

Naledi and Dineo finally reached the wide gate leading into the farm. They picked their way carefully across the metal strips of the cattle grid and Naledi lifted Dineo up for the last stretch of the journey, out of reach of the farm dogs. They were trained to snap and snarl at strangers and Naledi had taken careful note of how Nono managed to talk and calm them.

Usually when she came to this farm with Nono, Naledi was absorbed by the variety of trees and plants which flourished on either side of the long drive, great dark avocado trees, tangled clusters of mangoes, strong soaring paw-paw trees with green fruit already beginning to bulge up on high. But today as she walked anxiously up the drive, she saw only a picture of a great lorry driving up to their house and people forcing them onto it. To make it worse, in her picture, the father of her friend Poleng was standing by, casually watching.

CHAPTER 3

Turning the corner of the drive near the farmhouse, Naledi scanned the garden at the front of the long white house with its shaded cool verandah, green leaves and bright creeping flowers. Nono was nowhere to be seen. As Naledi was walking around the side of the house, the dogs suddenly came pelting towards her, barking wildly. A woman scrubbing a large pot in a sink outside the kitchen looked up. She shouted to the dogs, which seemed to calm them a little, called out a greeting to the girls, and pointed to where Nono was working. Beyond a revolving hose sprinkling water in great arcs across the neat grass and close to the shimmering blue swimming pool, was Nono, kneeling on all fours, searching the lawn for weeds. As soon as Dineo saw her she scrambled down and ran to her granny through a spray of water, calling, "Nono! Nono!" Startled, Nono turned and tried to push against the ground to heave herself up. Naledi hurried to help while Dineo clutched at her granny's skirt.

"Why have you come? Why are you not in school?" Her tired face was clouded with worry.

"It's something bad at home, Nono! A man is painting numbers on all the doors and two white men are there. They say we all have to go. They say lorries are coming soon."

"What?" As Nono's voice rose in exclamation, her body suddenly went limp and heavy and Naledi wasn't able to stop her grandmother from sinking back onto her knees. A worn hand shielded the wrinkled skin beneath her white head scarf. Naledi knelt down on the grass beside her.

"We can all refuse Nono! What can they . . ."

She stopped suddenly. The 'Missus' was approaching. Quickly she pulled herself up, nodding slightly.

The young white woman had her fair hair pulled back in a bun.

"What's going on here, Martha?"

Nono's hand uncovered her face but remained pressed into the sagging furrows of her cheek. She breathed deeply as if beginning to speak, but instead all that she managed was a sigh.

The woman turned to Naledi: "Why aren't you in school today?"

Naledi glanced down at her dress. It was her school uniform. Her mind had been in such turmoil, she hadn't really thought about what her normal day should have been.

"I had to bring my grandmother some news. It's bad news, Mi . . ."

Naledi lowered her voice at the end, so the last word 'Missus' was a mumble. She hated using that word. Most white people expected that a black person should say it to show their respect for them. Nono had already spoken to her about it as she had noticed how the word seemed to stick in her grand-daughter's throat. She had said that Naledi could get into a lot of trouble if she did not say it. In fact Nono herself might even lose her job if the white woman thought that her grand-daughter was too 'cheeky'. White people could sometimes be very fussy over a thing like that. It made them feel uneasy.

"What is it then?"

Nono put out a hand as if to silence Naledi and to be helped up. When she had struggled to her feet. Nono answered, but with her eyes turned away, fixed into the distance.

"The child says someone is putting numbers on our houses, Missus. They say we have to go somewhere else."

The white woman hesitated, smoothing back some stray hair.

"But didn't you know about this?"

Nono shook her head.

"Well, I don't think you should worry too much, Martha. I'm sure it'll work out all right in the end. It was planned a long time ago that all you black people should go to live together in your own place. You know, your own homeland just for yourselves. You're lucky it's not so far from here and they say there'll be buses. Maybe just a one or two hour ride, so you can still come here to work each day. Then at night you can go back to your own home."

Nono and Naledi were quite silent. Only Dineo moved, rubbing her back against Nono.

"Look, you don't have to worry! I'm prepared to wait for a couple of weeks after you move while you sort yourselves out. Then if you travel here on the bus, you can still have your job. You're a good girl, Martha, and I'd be sorry to lose you."

Very softly Nono replied, "Yes Missus."

"Listen, if the child helps you a bit now. I'll let you go early today. Just finish weeding this section of the lawn, hey?"

"Thank you Missus."

Nono's voice was still low and soft. Only Naledi heard its pain.

*

It was mid-afternoon when they reached the outskirts of the village, Nono leaning heavily on Naledi, Dineo trotting solemnly alongside. Usually the village would be fairly quiet at this time, but today people stood in twos and threes outside their houses. The large white numbers glistened brightly in contrast to the weathered browns of the doors, the walls and the earth. Even when a vast shadow fell over everything as a passing cloud blotted out the sun, the numbers stood out boldly.

As they approached a group of women, a voice called out.

"Dumela Mma! How is it with you?"

Without waiting for a reply, their relative Mma Kau hurried over to help support Nono for the rest of the journey home. Once inside, Nono was gently lifted onto the bed. Mma Kau promised to return later with a special herb drink. Dineo clambered onto the bed next to Nono.

As Naledi was turning on the little primus stove, Tiro came running into the house.

"It's also Boomdal! They're also going to move Boomdal! They put numbers there too! Your friend Taolo just told me."

Tiro breathlessly poured out this latest news to his sister. Boomdal was where they went to school. It was a township for black people near to the white town. A few years ago there had been disturbing rumours that the government wanted to get rid of Boomdal because it was 'too close' to the white town. But nothing happened, so everyone carried on as before.

A soft groan came from the bed and Tiro turned to see Nono lying there. Immediately he crossed the room to her.

"Intshwarele Nono! I'm sorry, I didn't see you there. Aren't you well, Nono?"

"It's nothing child. Tell us what the chief said to Mma Tshadi. Your sister told me you went to hear them." Nono's voice was weak.

Everyone knew that at the best of times Mma Tshadi and the chief didn't get on, in spite of being related. Mma Tshadi was certainly the most outspoken member of the village and she often commented on the chief's enjoyment of alcohol. Nothing much escaped her quick eye and tongue. Her most recent complaint was well known; that the chief didn't want to help her get a licence to extend the small shop she ran from her home. She used one tiny room in her house for supplies to sell to the villagers. Otherwise the nearest shops were an hour's walk away in Boomdal. But for over a year Chief Sekete had put off applying to the authorities for permission for her to build a larger room. Until now, others had put this down to the bad feeling between the two. No-one had thought that there might be another reason concerning them all.

Tiro drew in breath and began his report:

"When we got to the chief's house, Mma Sekete said her husband was still asleep. You should have seen Mma Tshadi's face! So Mma Sekete said she would get him up. When he came to the door he looked very angry to be woken. But after Mma Tshadi finished with him, he looked sick. He didn't say anything, only that he will hold a kgotla later this afternoon."

"Did you see Poleng?" Naledi asked quietly.

Tiro shook his head. Nono was breathing heavily.

"We used to trust our chief," she whispered.

CHAPTER 4

The sky which had been so clear and blue early that morning was grey and rumbling with thunder as Naledi and Tiro arrived late in the afternoon at the small church hall. They had left Nono at home asleep after drinking Mma Kau's herb mixture, with Dineo curled up beside her. Word had been sent round through the chief's messengers that this unexpected kgotla would take place in the church. It was usual to hold the kgotla in the open outside the chief's house, but with the likelihood of a heavy storm, the meeting place had been changed.

The hall was already crowded as Naledi and Tiro slipped through to where they could stand at the side.

It was a simple stone building in contrast to the wattle and mud houses of the village. The church had been constructed many years ago when Rra Rampou, one of the village elders, and the children's grandfather, Nono's husband, were young men. It had been the pride of the community since then. Inside were bare floor-boards, wooden benches and a table at one end. Today three chairs were placed beside the table on which stood a paraffin lamp waiting to be lit.

The air in the room was hot and sticky and agitation could be heard in people's voices. Usually before a thunder-storm bringing welcome rain, there would be a sense of expectancy, of relief. Instead, this afternoon, something ominous hovered over them all. As Naledi scanned faces in the dim light, she caught a glimpse of Poleng, standing at the back, almost out of sight. What would she say to her when they met? Even if her friend hadn't known about the removal, could they still be friends if Poleng's father had indeed agreed to it?

People moved aside to make way for Chief Sekete and two of his brothers. The Sekete brothers lived with their families near the city of Pretoria and only returned to the family home at Bophelong at Christmas and on special occasions. Chief Sekete must have asked them to come urgently for this special kgotla.

The chief moved forward. Naledi looked at him. He was a short stocky man, his bald head circled by a narrow band of greying hair. His forehead remained remarkably clear of lines, smoothly rounding over from his rather shiny head. As if in harmony with these contours, his ample stomach pulled at the buttons of his dark suit.

"Ba ga etsho . . . my people, this is a difficult time for us. As you know, sometimes the weather changes and we are forced to change our plans about how we shall plant or how we shall build. In the beginning we complain, but then sometimes we find that everything has worked out well. It isn't easy to see ahead . . ."

He paused, clearing his throat, but before he could continue Mma Tshadi stood up:

"None of us can say what the weather will be. Tonight we have not come to discuss the plans of the weather but the plans of the whites. Just tell us about these plans."

A murmur rippled through the room, supporting Mma Tshadi. An elderly man stood up. It was Rra Rampou:

"Pardon me if I speak out of turn, but I am very much disturbed. I have lived in this place since I was born. My father rented from your father and now they both rest under the earth in this place. This is where my body must rest when my time comes. So what we want to know is this: what do the numbers mean?"

As voices rose again the chief put up his hand. Outside there was a sudden crash of thunder, followed by the pelting of rain on the thatch above.

"I hadn't finished speaking when Mma Tshadi interrupted. I should remind you of our custom that a chief should have his say first. I was telling you that sometimes we have to change our plans. That is happening to us now. We are being asked to go and live in our own homeland."

"Hei! This land, right here, is our home! What 'homeland' are you talking about?"

This time Mma Tshadi did not even wait for the chief to pause before her question burst out.

"I am talking about Bophuthatswana – the place for people who speak Tswana."

"What about those here who speak other languages?" a deep voice boomed out from the back.

"They will be able to go to their own homelands." Chief Sekete didn't look directly at the speaker who had asked the question.

"What 'homelands' are these you talk about? People

are living peacefully together in their own homes right here, their fathers and mothers before them, even their grandparents. Why should they want another home?"

"Listen to reason, my people! We know these things have already been decided by the highest councils in the land by those with power. Surely it is better for us to accept . . ."

"Accept?" The deep voice resounded again from the back.

". . . *You* may wish to accept, but did you ask the opinion of anyone here?"

By now everyone was turning around to look at the speaker. He was standing at the back, a strikingly tall man with a thick black beard streaked with grey whom Naledi recognised as Taolo's father Saul. Yes, next to him was Taolo Dikobe, the boy who within the twelve months since his arrival had become the most outspoken student in their school. He was in the class above Naledi, but his reputation had spread rapidly throughout the school. This was the first time Taolo's father had come to a kgotla because the government had 'banned' him. It was well known that he was not allowed to talk with more than two people, otherwise the police would put him back in jail. Clearly he was taking a big risk this evening by ignoring the order.

Naledi had heard Taolo explain that his father had already spent ten years in prison for helping workers in their factories. The family then lived in Soweto. But as soon as his father came out of prison, the authorities had banished him to this remote village. Just before he had arrived, the white magistrate had come to warn the villagers about him. In fact, Poleng's father had translated the magistrate's words into Tswana, telling them how they would find themselves in trouble if they had anything to do with Saul Dikobe. Naledi remembered feeling uneasy at the time, but perhaps Chief Sekete had no choice except to pass on the magistrate's message.

Still the message had had its effect. People had kept clear of the Dikobe house, although they would greet Mma Dikobe when they saw her. She had a friendly smile and worked in the hospital where Naledi's Mma had taken Dineo when she was ill. Although Taolo was also popular in school, no-one visited him at home. In fact the only regular visitors to the house were policemen coming to check on Saul Dikobe, usually at night and disturbing the quiet of the whole village with the roaring of their vehicles.

Now, as Saul Dikobe's deep voice kept coming from the back, Chief Sekete took out his handkerchief and wiped his forehead, holding up his other hand for silence.

Suddenly he pointed straight at Saul Dikobe.

"You are a known trouble-maker, an agitator! You should not be here! If my people listen to you, things will go badly for them. Leave them alone!"

"Can a chief not trust his people to hear different voices? Are they children who must listen only to the words of their parents?"

Before Chief Sekete could reply, one of his brothers at the table interrupted:

"Let us not argue. This is a hard time for us all, so let my brother explain what he knows of this removal."

Naledi could see trickles of sweat on Chief Sekete's temple, glinting in the uneven light from the paraffin lamp on the table. An uneasy silence was now disturbed only by the angry, steady thudding of rain on the roof. Chief Sekete began again: He and his brothers, being the landowners, had known for a few months about plans for the removal. However they hadn't wanted to worry anyone else until the matter was fully settled. The magistrate had explained to them that all the villagers who were tenants paying rent were 'squatters' according to the law, so they had no right to stay, even if their parents had lived here before them. The chief had been taken to see where the village would be moved. Part of it had once been an area of white farms. The man from 'Affairs' had promised that the government would build houses for all the villagers before the removal.

A deep, dry laugh broke out from the back. It was Saul Dikobe again: "Do you know what they call 'a house'? Which sort did they tell you about? The one made of four pieces of tin with a roof, where you cook like meat when it's hot and shiver like ice when it's cold? Or the tomato-box made from wood which lets in the wind? My friends, let us ask our chief if he is going to be living in such a 'house'."

Chief Sekete steadied his hand on the table. People were waiting for his reply. No . . . his accommodation would be a little different. Because his family were landowners, they were to be given houses which had previously been occupied by white families, as 'compensation'.

"Hei!" Mma Tshadi's shout pierced the room, its high pitch seeming to shatter once and for all the customary behaviour at a kgotla. Questions now flooded forward. What about their crops already growing in the fields, ready for harvesting in a few months? What would they have to eat for the rest of the year if they had to leave these behind? Why were they called 'squatters'? What land would they have for planting? Where would they find work? Were there schools? Was there a hospital? Life was hard here, but at least they somehow kept alive. They were not ignorant and had heard how things were in the place now called 'Bop'. A few people had got rich there, but if you were poor, then it was only a place for dying.

As the questions and comments grew louder, Chief Sekete's brothers began to whisper urgently to each other. Raising his voice, the Chief announced that these were all matters which should rather be put to someone from the 'Affairs' department. He would see if a meeting could be arranged but for now, the kgotla was over. With that, almost pushing the Chief between them, his brothers elbowed their way through the crowd to the door. One of them stood by the entrance, urging everyone else to leave.

The yard outside the church-hall filled with bodies and voices, as people spilled out into the gathering dark, and scurried home in the steady drizzle. In the crowd Naledi held on to Tiro's shoulder, a hand over her head to ward off the rain.

"Naledi?"

She looked up through the rain, straight into the wet face of her friend Poleng, being jostled along next to her.

"Let me talk with you!" Poleng's voice had a pleading note to it.

Telling Tiro to go on ahead, Naledi moved sideways with Poleng through the crowd until they were able to run around to the side of the church for shelter.

"I didn't know, Naledi! Truly I didn't know!"

Poleng's voice was unsteady. Naledi wasn't sure whether her friend's face was wet only because of the rain.

"When did you find out?"

"Today. Just like you. When Mma Tshadi came to our house. I heard what was going on. My father wouldn't let me go to school after that." Poleng's voice was shaking slightly.

"What did your father tell you?" asked Naledi.

"He said it's better for us to move because we can never win against the government . . . they will just punish us all and make it much worse . . ."

Poleng paused, as if what she had to say next was difficult: "He also said . . . our family will have a nice house to live in . . . and he might send me . . . away to school."

"To boarding school? Where will he get the money?"

Naledi's shocked tone was too much for Poleng and she broke into sobs.

"I don't . . . know . . . That's . . . what he said . . . and on the way here, no-one would talk to me . . . they just gave me bad looks . . ."

Her friend's whole body was shivering. Poor Poleng, thought Naledi, pained and upset by what her father had done, but trapped. It wasn't her fault.

Naledi was just about to put her arm around Poleng when they saw a torch shining at them through the rain as someone hurried towards them. It was Chief Sekete with rain dripping off the edges of his umbrella.

"Poleng! What are you doing here? I told you to stay at home with your mother! Oh, it's you Naledi. You should also be at home. Tla re tsamayeng! . . . Come!"

Without waiting for a reply, Chief Sekete marched the girls across the yard and down the soaking track. No-one spoke, although Naledi wished she could say something to Poleng. It would have to wait. She felt awkward and angry to be walking next to Chief Sekete. Outside Nono's house, she quickly mumbled a reply to Chief Sekete's farewell. Poleng said nothing.

CHAPTER 5

Poleng did not appear for the walk to school the next day. Naledi waited a short while for her near Mma Tshadi's, but when her friend didn't arrive she realised that her father must be keeping her away again as Poleng had told her. Was he expecting trouble? Previously she would have quickly run down to Poleng's house to see what had happened, but now she didn't want to go near there and risk facing Chief Sekete. Naledi had wanted to stay at home herself to look after Nono, but her grandmother had insisted that the children shouldn't miss school.

"I'm just a little tired, that's all," she reassured them. "Mma Kau will look in. Your mother pays a lot for you to be in school, and already you missed it yesterday."

Not all the children from Bophelong went to school. Only those whose parents could afford to send them. They walked to Boomdal each morning in small clusters and pairs. Without hurrying, it took about an hour, first along the dirt-track, then taking a short-cut across the veld. Poleng had always walked with Naledi, chatting, joking, testing each other on homework. The time went quickly that way.

The primary school began earlier than the high school in order to fit in two sessions with different pupils, so Tiro had already gone on. As Naledi set off without Poleng, she kept a look out for Taolo Dikobe. Sometimes he would join them. Ever since he had arrived she had instinctively liked him, admiring the way he seemed not be afraid to say what he thought, even to the headmaster. Mr Molaba, the head, was not used to being contradicted and Taolo had soon received a number of beatings for being 'cheeky'. Yet each time he had emerged more angry and determined. When it came to being threatened with expulsion, his mother was called to the school. Word went round that Mrs. Dikobe had stood up for her son, telling Mr Molaba that she and his father hadn't encouraged their son to be 'cheeky' but simply to be honest and truthful. His father had gone to jail for ten years because of what he believed. If Taolo was being rude or impolite, then he should be punished. However, if he was merely expressing a different view from the teachers, then she saw nothing wrong in that. The headmaster had been quite taken aback. Parents, like most of his pupils up until now, usually submitted to him. According to

Taolo, Mr Molaba had looked close to explosion, ending the interview abruptly by telling his mother, "I shall give him a last chance. But you had better talk some sense into him if he wants to continue here."

Naledi had the feeling that Taolo liked her too, although the only time they really talked to each other was to and from school. When he had found out that she had been to Soweto and was writing to a friend in the thick of all the protests there, he had begun to speak openly about some of his feelings. It was clear that he bitterly missed his old home in Soweto. Yes, he and his friends had felt death could be around the corner. But in spite of informers, spies and armed police almost everywhere, they had been gripped by the excitement of being part of a great revolt against apartheid. Whenever Taolo said that word, he spat it out. It was apartheid that ruled and destroyed their lives. The banishment order on his father had come as a shock. Taolo said he had been so eager for the return of his father – an honoured survivor of ten years on 'The Island' after a year in jail awaiting trial – that he had blinkered himself to what was likely to happen next. After release from prison, his father hadn't even been allowed a night in their Soweto home. The police had escorted him immediately to Bophelong. Since the banning order prevented his father from working, the family continued to rely on Mrs Dikobe's income. Fortunately she had managed to arrange a transfer from the large hospital near Soweto to the small country hospital where she worked now. So the family had at last been reunited in this remote village after eleven years apart.

Taolo found himself torn. He desperately wanted to be back with all his friends in the hub of all the action in Soweto, but he also wanted to be with his father. He had so few memories of being with him at all before the age of five when they had been parted. With all his political work, Saul Dikobe's time with his family had always been scarce. Nor had prison weakened him. His mind seemed stronger than ever. Taolo had felt this strength even through the prison bars. For the final three years of his father's sentence, he had been allowed to accompany his mother on her yearly visit to Robben Island. It was known as the most terrible of prisons where the authorities sent those whom they thought the most dangerous – to be locked in not only by bars and walls, but by a whole sea.

Once, when Poleng had been ill, and it was just the two of them walking to school, Naledi had asked Taolo to describe it. Some part inside her was driving her to know more about these things. He had been quiet for a while as if deciding how to answer, then in a voice far quieter and softer than usual, his words had enabled Naledi to draw a vivid picture in her mind: "We went by train right across the country to Cape Town. It's so far you have to sleep while sitting on the train. Then they take you by boat to the island. Hey, I tell you, those waves are rough! They turn your stomach upside down. In front of you is the grey rocky island. It's so bare you can't believe that people live there. Hardly anyone speaks. All you can think about are the people locked away in the middle of such a terrible sea. Inside the visiting room, you wait a long time in a small cubicle for them to bring the prisoner. There's a telephone next to a window with bars and very thick glass. My father had to speak through the telephone on his side. Each time you could see his hair was getting more grey but he was still so tall and upright with his eyes smiling. He must have hidden all his pain. He would say, We're doing fine in here!' Not 'I am', but 'We are' – always showing that he and the other political prisoners hadn't given up their struggle together. Small things like that help you not to give up but to get on with the fight."

Walking by herself up the muddy dirt-track out of the village, Naledi was reminded of those words as she thought about the kgotla and how Saul Dilobe had talked to the chief. What would the government do if someone like Taolo's father were their chief and he refused to go along with them?

"Naledi!"

She stopped and turned. It was Taolo sprinting up the track.

"Where's your friend? Is she hiding her face again today?" His voice had a bitter edge.

Naledi's instinct was to defend Poleng after their brief meeting.

"She can't help what her father does. She's upset."

"So, she's got problems. We all have."

He paused and aimed his foot at a small stone in his path. It hurtled out of the way.

"First they kick our family out of Soweto and now they want to kick everyone out of here."

"So what can we do?"

"Fight back of course. My father says that in a few places the people are still on their land, although they were told to leave long ago. They made their plans together and stayed firm."

"But if we refuse they'll come with dogs and guns – and what do we have to fight back with?"

"Look sis, in Soweto children have been resisting with just their hands and stones against trucks, tanks with fully armed police and soldiers. Okay, so they keep killing us, but they still didn't break us. Even more people are on our side now. Parents see what the police are doing to their children and they also join in the struggle. We're getting stronger all the time."

Naledi didn't reply. Taolo spoke like a town boy, calling her 'sis', often teasing her too. But today there was no fun in his voice. He was deadly serious. A picture came to her mind. Their homes surrounded by soldiers and tanks . . .

"There's not just one way of fighting," Taolo continued as if reading her mind. "We can check the law.

Maybe we'll find something there, some bit they forgot to fix properly. Then we can use that. They always shout to the world about 'law and order'! Everything – even their killing – is done by the law, tch!"

As Taolo spoke on and Naledi listened – about newspapers, campaigns and getting others to support them – it all began to seem possible. Maybe they could, one way or another, stop the government's plan! The first, most important thing was to be well organised. In Boomdal people had formed their own Residents' Association some time ago. That showed they did not trust the councillors appointed by the white commissioner. Taolo said that the villagers of Bophelong should have followed their example. Instead they had continued to put all their trust in one person who was being paid by the white authorities, Chief Sekete.

"If Sekete doesn't do what the whites want, they sack him. So he tries to please them!"

Although she still did not say anything, inwardly Naledi knew what Taolo was saying about her friend's father was true.

"We must do the same as Boomdal and join with them. To hell with Sekete!" he continued, looking directly at Naledi. 'What do you say, sis?"

Her eyes had been fixed steadily on the path and the grey grass on either side as they walked. Without stopping, she now turned her face to him sharply.

"Go siame! All right! So how do we start?"

CHAPTER 6

As they walked through the high wire gates into the school grounds, there was no time to talk to other students. Across the bare yard stood the single-story grey brick buildings with flat iron roofs, containing the classrooms, staffroom and head teacher's office. There was no hall. The only shade in the yard was under a couple of trees near the head's office.

The whistle had been blown and the classes were lining up as Naledi and Taolo slipped into their places. Mr Molaba was standing on the steps overseeing the operation as if he were a military commander. All that was missing was the cap. A large man with small eyes and broad cheeks, he had deep lines which seemed to pull at his mouth. Barking the number of each class in turn, he watched with an eagle eye as the students marched away. It was unwise to look slipshod as one of his favourite pastimes was making a class spend their whole break period tramping up and down the playground in strict left-right fashion.

Straight after registration it was time for assembly so within five minutes they were marching back to the yard. Again Mr Molaba waited, stiff and impatient, as the last students trooped back and the shuffling stopped. He cleared his throat with a cough:

"I have an announcement before our prayers today. You all know by now that you and your families are due to move from here in the very near future. I have not yet received information abut the school you will be able to attend in the homeland, but I should like to warn all of you to behave well in your last few weeks at this school. It may even be that you and I will meet again in your next school . . ."

Mr Molaba paused, looking down at rows of faces.

"In any event, all school records will be kept up to date until your very last day here, before they are sent on. So those of you who have been thinking this period might provide a good opportunity for mischief, should think again."

Naledi could not be sure, but Mr Molaba's gaze

seemed to focus on Taolo. Without moving her head too obviously she glanced at him. Taolo's eyes were targetted on the headmaster, steady and unmoving.

In the arithmetic lesson that followed with Mr Gwala, Naledi found it difficult to concentrate. She was not the only one. Other students were fidgeting and restless too. How could you keep your mind on long multiplication when there were so many more important questions to be answered? Why did Mr Molaba make that remark about being in their next school? Was he to be made its headmaster? Naledi felt sure he knew more than he had said. He had made it all sound so matter-of-fact with 'your next school'. Obviously he accepted the removal. As it was, he was already better off than most people. Perhaps he had also been promised one of the houses which had previously belonged to the white people, so long as he made no objections. Naledi clicked to herself in disgust, but the sound carried and she was soon aware of her teacher looking at her. She tried to change the grimace which she felt must be on her face.

"What is it Naledi? You don't seem to be working hard today."

As Naledi stood up wondering what to say to Mr Gwala, an idea flew through her mind. Dare she try it? Why not? Mr Gwala was more approachable than most of the teachers.

"Sir," she began hesitantly, "where will you go if they force Tswanas into the place they say is our 'homeland'?"

The class was completely silent, all eyes on the teacher. Everyone knew that although he spoke Tswana fluently, Mr Gwala's first language was Zulu. Mr Gwala glanced a little nervously towards the open door. The headmaster had an unpleasant habit of springing upon a class in a way that kept his teachers even more alert than their pupils.

"Well, Naledi . . . since you ask, I have to tell you that

I don't know. This business is as much a shock to me as it must be to all of you. I know that non-Tswanas aren't welcome in Bop so I wouldn't be able to teach there for sure. If we are forced from here, the only place I could get a teaching job would be far away in KwaZulu."

"Do you want to go there, sir?" asked the boy next to Naledi.

"I haven't been there since my grandparents died when I was a child. My parents made their home here in the Transvaal," the teacher replied quietly.

For a few seconds no-one said a word. It would be too personal to ask Mr Gwala to explain. Then a girl put up her hand.

"What is it Miriam?"

The girl stood.

"Sir, my mother speaks Tswana but my father's first language is Sotho. They have been living here together in Boomdal for twenty years. What will happen to them now?"

The girl looked down all the time she was speaking, struggling to keep her voice steady.

"I honestly don't know Miriam."

A shape at the door blotted out light.

"Is anything wrong Mr Gwala?"

Mr Molaba's harsh voice startled everyone and eyes hurriedly turned down to books and pencils. Before Miriam could sit down, however, the headmaster asked her to bring up her work. She walked slowly forward, book in hand. Mr Molaba glanced at the almost empty page.

"Is this all you have done this morning?"

He glanced at the sums on the board.

"You are in Standard Seven and you cannot do long multiplication? I think you had better present yourself outside my office every break-time this week so that you can learn. Don't you agree Mr Gwala?"

Naledi thought she heard a mocking tone in the

headmaster's voice. He didn't wait for Mr Gwala to reply.

"If there are any others who do not complete the work that has been set, you can see them at break-time yourself . . . can you not, Mr Gwala?"

This time, the mockery was clear. Naledi glanced at their teacher, feeling embarrassed for him. She could not make out his eyes. Did they show hurt, or a quiet dignity? How she hated Mr Molaba and all those like him who enjoyed crushing others. But there was no time for emotion. Mr Gwala was telling the class that they had five minutes to finish all the sums. All sorts of murmurings and sighs were followed by intense concentration with heads down, when the sounds changed to those of surprise and relief. Mr Gwala was writing the answers into their correct spaces on the board!

"Hurry up!" was all he said.

By the time the bell rang, everyone except Miriam had completed the task. As they escaped into the playground, they saw Mr Gwala walking with her towards the head's office. Perhaps he was not going to let her walk into the lion's den alone.

*

At the back of the building furthest from the headmaster's office Naledi found a crowd of students already around Taolo. His voice was bitter and angry: "They take six pieces of land and put some dummy 'President' in charge. It doesn't even matter that the bits of land don't even all join up. Then they say, 'These pieces aren't South Africa any more. From now on we say they are Bophuthatswana and any Tswanas we don't want, we send them there.' Then they take a few more pieces somewhere else and say, 'These are KwaZulu and they'll do for the Zulus . . . and the Xhosas can have these slices over here', and so on. Any fool can see how they want to split us up! They want to force us back to the days of our great grandfathers, pushing us here and there, keeping us apart so they can control us! Divide and rule! Hell man, the *whole* of South Africa belongs to us – all of us! Why shouldn't we be free to make our homes wherever we choose, live with whoever we want? I ask you what good is there in that place they call our 'homeland'?"

"But some people say it's better there in Bop, that blacks are at least free to get to the top instead of always being under some white boss."

It was one of the older Boomdal students who spoke, his voice sharp and confident. Taolo replied quickly to the challenge:

"What do you mean 'free'? This Chief they made 'President' must still say, 'Yes sir, no sir,' to big white chief Botha. Look, it's Botha who pays his salary! I tell you the only 'freedom' in Bop is for the 'President' and his friends to make money for themselves and . . .!"

"It's true!" a girl intervened angrily in a high-pitched voice. "My father's sister was forced to Bop. All her life she had lived in Potchefstroom. Then one day the police came, broke the houses, pushed everyone onto trucks and cleared the whole place. They dumped my aunty in Rooigrond." Pausing to suck in a breath, the speaker threw open the palms of her hands, as if at a loss to find the words she needed.

"Do you know what Rooigrond is? It's . . . it's just dry red earth, no fields, no grass. To begin the people just had tents. At her home my aunty had land to plough and animals. But the cows died on the trucks and the police forced her to leave the pigs. Maybe the whites took them but she didn't get any money. There's nothing at Rooigrond. The ploughs and hoes are still rusting on the ground. People are starving there now. Is that 'freedom'?"

As the girl spoke, Naledi felt as if a belt were being tightened and pulled across her chest, trapping her. It was no good just listening to these terrible stories. They had to *do* something. Her voice rang out without her planning it.

"We must refuse to go! All of us must refuse!"

With shouts of agreement coming from all sides, Taolo started again: "In Soweto the students got their parents to take action. If we organise we can do the same here. In Boomdal you have a committee but in Bophelong there's . . ."

"SO!"

Without warning, Mr Molaba's voice thundered through the gathering, students peeling backwards as he marched between them.

"So! We have our young agitator at work, caught red-handed with his brave gang!" He glowered at Taolo. "Your mother won't be able to get you out of this one so easily. It'll be the police she'll be seeing next, not me! Clearly you are quite determined to ignore my instructions!"

Taolo remained silent, but returned Mr Molaba's stare, eyeball to eyeball, until the headmaster jerked his head away letting his eyes rove across the whole group. His voice leaped suddenly.

"I WILL NOT HAVE POLITICS DISCUSSED IN MY SCHOOL! I have told you before and I repeat it. I will NOT tolerate anyone bringing politics into these grounds, ESPECIALLY when that person has a known trouble-maker for a father!"

For a split second it seemed as if Taolo was going to lunge at the headmaster and hit him, but quick protective hands and arms held him back.

"We are only talking about our own lives! You shouldn't stop us."

Again Naledi was taken by surprise to hear her own voice.

" 'Shouldn't'? You, a pupil in my school, think you can tell me what I 'shouldn't' do? I see that Dikobe the young agitator has had some success already. Go siame!

Well, we shall see how much you want to follow in his footsteps when I'm finished. Both of you go to my office. As for the rest, get to your classes immediately and stop playing at being grown-ups. You are playing with fire!"

CHAPTER 7

For a long time afterwards Naledi couldn't think about what followed in the headmaster's office without reliving the intense humiliation. She felt as if nothing would ever wipe out the memory of the conflicting dismay and anger that arose inside her when Mr Molaba pulled out his thin cane, bending it casually with his hands to check its flexibility. Satisfied, he swung a chair into the middle of the room and pointed to Naledi to bend over it. As she hesitated, Taolo remonstrated loudly,

"This is barbaric! You won't change anything by beating her! In Soweto students are boycotting their schools to stop this bullying with canes!"

"You are not in Soweto here! You don't seem able to get that straight!"

At that, Mr Molaba strode across to the door and instructed Miriam, who was still outside struggling with her sums, to call the four biggest boys in the top class to come immediately. On presenting themselves, they were ordered to take hold of Taolo's arms. Looking uneasy, they nevertheless did what they were told.

"They are restraining you in case you have any ideas of interfering with the discipline of this school," Mr Molaba said brusquely to Taolo. "I don't intend to beat *you* this time. You are beyond that and your punishment is to be more severe. However, I intend that you first witness the result of your work in agitating students in my school."

It all seemed hopeless to Naledi, but she managed to flash a defiant 'I won't give in' look to Taolo as she stretched over the chair. Taolo tried to shake the arms off him.

"Let go of me! I won't trouble this coward. Let's all watch a big grown man beat up a fifteen-year-old girl just because he doesn't like what she says."

The four students relaxed their grip slightly without taking their hands away. Their headmaster was still someone to be reckoned with. The cane sliced the air and pain bit into Naledi's body. Fiercely gripping the wooden-bar of the chair, she prayed that each searing, burning stroke would be the last. With her teeth clenched and her face screwed tightly into her arm-pit, she forced back the tears . . . three . . . four . . . oh God . . . five . . . six . . . wasn't that it? . . . oh help me . . . seven, eight, nine, ten . . . her scream would surely force its way out with the next slash. But the eleventh stroke didn't come. Instead Mr Molaba was ordering her to pull herself up and stand properly. Her legs were limp and her head was throbbing. As she attempted to straighten her clothes, she felt as if she no longer had proper control of her hands.

"Now let that be a lesson to you and to everyone else in this school. You may be a girl and all your work may be Grade A standard, but if you or any other pupil think you can ignore my authority, you know what to expect. I hope you have learnt what comes of listening to trouble-makers. Do you understand me?"

Naledi was aware that the headmaster was waiting for her to answer him but she kept silent, biting on her lower lip. She was not going to talk against Taolo now or ever. The Dikobes were right. You had to struggle.

"You have until tomorrow morning to come with

your reply to me, otherwise you risk the same fate as this 'hero' of yours." Mr Molaba turned to Taolo:

"I don't expect for one moment that you've been changed by seeing the suffering you've caused this girl who was foolish enough to listen to you. I am expelling you from this school for gross indiscipline. I shall give you a letter for your parents and my decision is final. There's no point in your mother coming to see me again. I shall be informing the Department and the Inspector immediately."

Taolo said nothing, and just stared straight ahead of him. His face showed neither shock nor indignation. Only a slight movement of his lips seemed to suggest contempt. But it was the expressions of the other four students that surprised Naledi as she glanced up at them. They looked even more ill at ease than before and there was no sign of ridicule. Were they embarrassed, ashamed?

With Taolo still waiting for his letter of expulsion, Mr Molaba dismissed the rest. Naledi had to force her wobbly legs to walk straight, but once outside Miriam was there and took her arm, helping her to the tap. As she scooped a few mouthfuls, the tingling water on her face relieved for a few seconds the smarting, stabbing pains through her body. Then Miriam led her to the back of one of the buildings where she could lean against a wall without being seen from the classrooms.

"We can wait here until you feel okay," Miriam spoke softly.

"Don't you . . . have to stay . . . outside his office?"

"I don't care anymore. I could hear everything inside! You stood up to him so why shouldn't I? Anyway what's the point . . . there'll be no more school for me soon." Bitterly she went on. Usually shy and retiring, Miriam now poured out in her quiet voice a turmoil of fears. If they were moved and Boomdal was destroyed, their father would lose his job in the Boomdal location office and they'd have no money. Non-Tswanas were not welcome in Bop and her father was Sotho so how would they manage. Even if a school accepted her and her sisters and brothers because their mother was a Tswana-speaker, the family would not be able to afford schooling any more.

"What have we done to them? Why can't they leave us here in peace?"

As Naledi listened, the aching in her body seemed to merge with the despair in Miriam's voice. She felt it pushing her downwards, making her feel weak and helpless. She forced herself away from the wall.

"But we don't have to give in! If we learn to stick together we can fight them! Look, after school we'll talk with Taolo. Molaba can't stop us doing that."

Clasping herself with her arms folded tightly and still bent slightly forward, Naledi began to walk in the direction of her classroom.

"I'll be all right now." Bit by bit she straightened herself up as they approached the classroom block. She would not let Mr Molaba have the pleasure of seeing her in pain.

CHAPTER 8

As students crowded out through the gates at the end of lessons, Naledi found arms on her shoulders and words of sympathy coming from all sides. Everyone knew what had happened and she was being congratulated for standing up to Mr Molaba. But the episode was not finished. He had said he would give her until the next day to promise to obey his rules, or face expulsion herself. He didn't seem to care about the high quality of her school work and her excellent exam marks. Although she grinned shyly at some of the remarks being made now, she was feeling cold inside.

"We shouldn't let him get away with it! He thinks he can just expel someone . . . as easy as that. We should do something to make him take Taolo back!"

"He won't listen even if we just want to speak to him."

". . . and the Inspector will back him up."

"Why don't we boycott? Like in Soweto!"

"What can that do? They already want to shut the school so they can move us."

Every avenue seemed blocked. The honking of a horn disturbed them suddenly. Mr Molaba, in his black Ford, was about to drive out through the gates and they were blocking the road outside. As they dispersed to either side, he put his head out of the window:

"What are you still doing here? If you want to stay on after school, I can arrange for you to do some useful work cleaning the yard!"

He drove deliberately slowly, watching until the students began to move down the road, breaking into twos and threes.

Naledi walked slowly, wondering whether Taolo had already taken his letter of expulsion to his mother at the hospital and whether he would come back past the school. A cow came ambling towards her, pursued by a young boy with a stick in his hand. She looked along the rutted road, past a patch of open ground tufted with dusty grey stubble, up to a white-washed building, the general store where you could buy anything from sugar to a pair of shoes. Scanning the figures relaxing against the wall of the store, she could not help feeling a little disappointed. It was silly of course, she knew. There were far more important things for Taolo to think about than how she had survived the beating. From Grace's letters about what was happening in Soweto she knew that people were getting hurt all the time, and their friends had simply to go on. There wasn't time to stop.

Joining the small trail of students on the path for Bophelong, Naledi missed Poleng. For how long did Chief Sekete intend to keep her away from school? Perhaps he would not let her return at all. Naledi spoke very little on the way home, too many conflicting thoughts racing through her head. What was she to answer Mr Molaba? If she were expelled what would be the effect on Nono? She had never seen her grandmother as weak and ill as this before. Another shock might be too much for her. Yet how was Nono going to survive being forced out of her own home? Somehow they *had* to stop the removal. She must see Taolo and his father. The way he had spoken at the meeting showed he understood exactly what they were up against.

Naledi was so deep in thought as they approached their village that although she was aware of the rumbling of a car, she didn't look up at it until it was practically on them. It was travelling fast over the ruts in the road, coming from the direction of Bophelong. Someone grabbed her arm, pulling her aside from the road. She peered up just in time to see the blue car from the day before and, to her shock, Poleng's face looking anxiously out from the back window. Among the cluster of heads she glimpsed Poleng's father and mother. Poleng threw her a final agonized glance.

"Hei! Where are they off to in such a hurry?" asked the older Sadire boy, David, who had snatched her from the road. He directed the question to Naledi. He was a neighbour and like everyone else knew that she and Poleng were like sisters.

"I don't know . . . but look there!"

They could now see the Sekete house and a small crowd gathering in front of it. In spite of aching limbs, Naledi ran forward with the others. Suddenly she saw her brother emerge out of the knot of people.

"What's happening?" She was breathless when she reached him. The curtains were drawn behind the closed windows of Poleng's house and the door was padlocked. "The white man came to take the chief away. They took cases with them."

Mma Tshadi's strong voice took over:

"I will tell you young people from the High School something else so you can tell it to those who are not here. Our chief has deserted us. He has betrayed us and he is frightened. So he needs the white man to protect him. That is why he asked the white man to take him and his family away. He will go to the big house he has been promised in our 'homeland'. But first, I am sure they will build a great fence around his new house. Is that not strange? A chief should protect his people. But now he wants protection from them!" Mma Tshadi's laugh was bitter.

Apart from the children, the crowd was made up largely of older women and a couple of elderly men, including Rra Rampou who leant heavily on his stick, as if anchoring himself to the ground. In her haste, Naledi did not immediately notice the newcomer hovering in the background. He was a young man with folded arms and a checked cap jutting over his forehead, shading his face. Only when David Sadire cried, "Jerry," did Naledi recognise him as the son Mma Kau had been anxiously waiting to return from his first contract on the gold mines. But could one year have made such a difference? Something in his manner was changed. He seemed aloof, almost unfamiliar, as he and David exchanged greetings. Although they were very different, as boys they had been so close – Jerry mischievous and buoyant, David much quieter but ever loyal. They had been inseparable companions until Jerry had unexpectedly dropped out of school to sign up for Egoli, the city of gold which stretched out its claws, hungry for young men to descend into its stomach. Now, as Naledi watched them, Jerry

Kau gave only half his attention to his former friend. What appeared to absorb him more was what the old people were saying. He listened intently as Mma Tshadi turned to Naledi.

"Tell that young friend of yours, Dikobe's son, to come and see me. All the words his father spoke last night were true. Perhaps he can advise us. They told us to keep away from him but look how we have been cheated already!"

"Yes Mma, I'll ask him to come to you tonight."

It was a relief. At least something was beginning to happen. If Rra Dikobe and Mma Tshadi got together, they would make the backbone of a strong team. Naledi called Tiro:

"Tla re tsamaye! Let's go! We must see how Nono is."

Replying with a quick nod her brother bent down, and before Naledi knew what he was about, he had picked up a stone and hurled it towards one of the windows of the Sekete house. It hit the metal frame and he swore. He would have tried again if Naledi had not grabbed him, forcing him into a swift walk home. It was worrying that Mma Kau had not been amongst the small crowd. Perhaps she had stayed behind with Nono because their grandmother was worse.

CHAPTER 9

It was as Naledi feared. Nono was lying on the bed, quite still, her eyes and cheeks sunken into the deep contours of her face. Mma Kau was sitting on a nearby chair, Dineo snuggled down quietly on her lap. The little girl, usually so full of life, seemed subdued. Standing by the bed, Naledi gently held her grandmother's hand. Nono's eyes slowly opened, gazed at Naledi and then closed again. That little movement seemed an enormous effort for her.

Going outside with Mma Kau, Naledi spoke in a whisper.

"I'll go to Mma Dikobe. Perhaps she can help."

Banning order or no banning order, she would go to the previously forbidden house. Mma Dikobe was a nurse. She had always looked friendly and surely would not refuse to help. Anyway, hadn't she, Naledi, promised Mma Tshadi to get a message to Taolo?

Mma Kau readily agreed to Naledi's suggestion.

"I see your son has returned, Mma. You must be very happy to have him back," Naledi added before leaving.

A slow smile lit up Mma Kau's broad face:

"Yes," she replied with a quiet pride. "He went away a boy but he has come back a man."

*

Houses in Bophelong were spread well apart and the authorities had placed the Dikobes in one of the remotest of them. Naledi approached it up the sloping track at the western end of the village. It was a small square thatched building which looked as if it had been freshly white-washed, surrounded by the same hard soil as all the other houses. At the side there was a patch where vegetables were growing. In the front yard stood a couple of young fruit trees tied to stakes. Keeping all these plants watered must be Taolo's responsibility, as Naledi had seen him come to the tap with a number of buckets which he pulled on a small hand-cart. After Dineo's illness, Nono had also tried to keep a small vegetable patch in their yard. With the soil being so dry, it had been extremely hard work to produce just a few rows of beans and spinach. Then, when the crop was almost ready for picking, a neighbour's goat had got through the makeshift fence of branches. Most of the crop was gone by the time they discovered him and Nono had said they would have to save up for a better fence before planting again beside the house.

Walking up to the Dikobe's house, Naledi saw that they had protected their patch with wire-netting. There was no sign of anyone outside and the door was closed although one of the windows was slightly open. Before she had time to knock, the door opened and Taolo stepped out, forcing her to move back a couple of paces.

"I can't ask you in so we'll have to talk here. Three makes a banned gathering you know!" He seemed to spit out the last sentence like a sour fruit.

"You mean they watch all the time?" Naledi's tone revealed her shock. The meaning of a banning order didn't really sink in when you only heard about it.

"You don't know when they're watching. That's their game, they keep you in suspense all the time."

"But I'm not coming to see your father. I want to see your mother and you."

"You tell that to the police and see if they believe you!"

While they were speaking, Taolo's eyes wandered past Naledi as if he were scanning the area. The only other house in sight was Rra Thopi's. His manner was casual, as if all this was a routine operation.

"Look . . . I'm sorry about what happened to you today. You could have apologized to Molaba and got out of it, but I'm glad you stood up to him. Now at least you understand a little more what to expect when you start resisting those with power."

For a split second Naledi was confused between pleasure at what seemed a compliment and a slight annoyance at Taolo's words, "Now at least you understand a little more". He seemed to know so much and made her realize she was just a beginner in these matters. She changed the subject.

"I came to ask if your mother will come to see my

grandmother. She's very ill . . . ever since she heard the news. My other message is for you from Mma Tshadi. She wants you to visit her right away. Chief Sekete has packed his cases and gone with his family. Mma Tshadi thinks your father can help."

Taolo grinned:

"So your chief has finally shown himself up! Mma and I came straight here from the hospital. We didn't see or hear anything. But I'm sorry about your grandmother. I'll call my mother for you right away."

Naledi stared around her while she waited, wondering from where the police could spy. Soon Mma Dikobe came out and greeted Naledi.

"Taolo has told me about you. I'm pleased you came. Give me a minute and I'll collect my bag with a few things I might need for your grandmother."

She gave a warm smile as she turned and disappeared into the house. She was shorter than her son with her rich brown face framed by attractive small black curls. Naledi could see she and Taolo shared the same features – high cheek bones under wide steady eyes. However her eyes seemed gentler and more tolerant than Taolo's which were often mocking and hard.

Taolo accompanied Naledi and his mother through the village until they came to the church. There he branched off to Mma Tshadi's. He had openly repeated to his mother the message Naledi had brought and she had simply nodded in silence. Naledi wished she could go with Taolo. It was so important for them all. This was the beginning of trying to fight the government's plans. But more immediately there was Nono to think about.

Mma Dikobe sat down next to Nono, and spoke softly, saying why she had come. She took Nono's temperature and held her wrist. Mma Kau and the children looked on anxiously as she explained how she could feel Nono's pulse. Her careful checks revealed that Nono's blood pressure was very high. Together

Mma Dikobe and Mma Kau gently sponged Nono and changed her clothes.

"It helps to feel a little fresher," Mma Dikobe said as she finally tucked in the blanket.

Nono seemed to murmur something.

"Don't strain yourself Mma," Taolo's mother said quietly. "Just lie here and have plenty of rest to get back your strength. I have some tablets to help you and something for you to drink. Even if you don't feel like eating, you must still please drink."

Producing a small bottle and a couple of packets from her bag. Mma Dikobe turned to Naledi:

"I'll show you how to follow these instructions to make each large spoon of this powder into soup. It has vitamins in it so it will help your granny get stronger. You must make sure that she keeps drinking and that she takes these tablets."

Mma Kau wanted to make Mma Dikobe some tea before she left, but she insisted on getting back home. It was rapidly getting dark. She promised, however, to call in and see Nono the following day. When she had gone, Mma Kau offered to stay the night with Nono and the children, but Naledi assured her that it was not necessary. Nono now seemed to be resting more peacefully and Mma Kau's son who had just returned from the mines would surely be missing her.

"Well, just you call me if you need me," Mma Kau stressed as she left their yard.

Mma Kau had even prepared them some food. Dineo had already eaten and was ready to go to sleep.

"Please can I sleep with Nono?" she begged.

"No Neo, Nono needs to rest," explained her sister.

"I won't wriggle, I promise!"

"Look, Nono's sick."

"Let her come, it's all right," came a whisper from the bed. Before Naledi could say any more, Dineo had skipped across the room and nestled down in the bed with Nono.

Naledi lit the paraffin lamp, then dished out two plates of pap and morogo, the wild spinach that grows even in the veld. She and Tiro sat eating in silence so Nono would not be disturbed. It was only when the lamp was out and they had settled down onto their mats in the small room at the side, that Tiro asked Naledi what had been happening at her school. There was no door between them and the main room so he kept his voice to a low whisper. He had heard talk of Naledi's beating when he had gone to collect the evening's water at the village tap. One of the students from the secondary school was there and had asked him if his sister had recovered.

"Why didn't you tell me?" Tiro's muffled voice sounded upset.

"There wasn't time. We were at the chief's place and then I had to get Mma Dikobe."

"Then tell me now."

Tiro didn't interrupt as Naledi spoke but when she had finished, he sounded even more upset.

"I'd like to get that headmaster and give him a thrashing like he gave you!" he whispered fiercely. He turned over violently to face the wall. Naledi put her hand out to his shoulder but he shook it away. With a sigh, she turned over to sleep.

CHAPTER 10

Naledi must have been sleeping lightly because the sound of footsteps running past the house woke her. She would probably have simply gone back to sleep if she had not noticed a strange glow through the thin curtains. Normally the village would be completely quiet and very dark unless the moon was up. But lifting the curtain, Naledi was shocked to see gigantic flames leaping into the black sky over in the direction of Poleng's house. She shook Tiro urgently and the two of them stared in stunned silence. The rest of the village seemed to be asleep while the eerie light spread its tentacles into the surrounding dark. Then one or two squares of light began to flicker in the distance and a couple of shadowy figures emerged in a neighbouring yard. Tiro begged to go outside and a whispered argument followed.

"I want to see what's happening."

"No. If the police come, there'll be trouble."

"How can the police come so soon?"

"I don't know, but you're staying here."

"Who did it? Who do you think?"

When Naledi gave no reply, Tiro added: "I'm glad his house is burning! He doesn't care if we lose *our* homes!"

"Don't talk like that! You'll get yourself into trouble with your big mouth."

Tiro dismissed the remark with a sucking noise. Naledi thought about Poleng as her eyes were riveted to the flames. Thank goodness she had gone. Would whoever set fire to the house have started it if the family had been inside? Perhaps the Chief had known this might happen. But who would actually do this? None of the older people she knew and which of the younger ones would be so daring? It must be someone brimming and burning with anger. It couldn't possibly be Taolo, could it? It wasn't the sort of thing he'd do, was it? Naledi's mind felt numb, repeating the question to herself. She said nothing to Tiro.

*

With the sky beginning to lighten, Naledi took Nono a

glass of water, gave her a couple more of Mma Dikobe's pills and checked that she was comfortable. Dineo was still sleeping soundly as the two older children slipped quietly outside. It was usual for them to leave early to collect the day's water from the village tap. But today instead of heading towards the tap near the church, they ran in between the mud walls and wire fences of neighbouring brown-earth yards in the direction of the chief's house.

Others were already there, staring at blackened, charred and smoking walls, roofless and open to the sky. The dark, twisted metal of the padlock that had secured the house yesterday now hung limply from what remained of the door frame. The door itself had disappeared into the heaps of scattered debris and smouldering ashes. Slowly Naledi edged towards the window of the bedroom where Poleng used to sleep. She could feel the heat through the thin soles of her shoes. Standing on tip-toes all she could see through the haze of smoke was the metal of bed frames. Tiro came up beside her and even he looked shaken now. This was something bigger than throwing stones.

Naledi stepped backwards, away from the ring of heat. A voice in the gathering had mentioned the word 'police'. That seemed to bring her to her senses. Yes, the police would soon be here, asking questions. There was already another question she had not yet decided how to answer, and Mr Molaba was expecting a reply today. She had pushed that matter right out of her mind, as if she could get rid of it that way! Should she give him an apology she did not mean, or risk being expelled? She should have asked Taolo what he thought. But no . . . she should not rely so much on him. Sometimes he could be very brusque, as if telling her that she should make up her own mind. In any case if he'd had anything to do with burning down the chief's house, he would have gone into hiding.

But she needed to talk to someone. Suddenly Naledi knew who it was. Mma Dikobe, who seemed so calm yet determined. She had promised to call in on Nono, but perhaps that wouldn't be until after she returned from work. Naledi did not want to trouble her at home again, especially before work when people were always rushing. Go siame . . . all right, she would just stay at home with Nono today, however much her grandmother protested. She would offer to take a message to the farm to say that Nono was ill and Mma Kau would also be able to get some free time to spend with her son. Let Mr Molaba wait!

Naledi need not have worried about what excuse to make to Nono about not going to school. While they were waiting to fill their buckets at the tap the police arrived. A distant roar coming closer focussed all eyes through the early light towards the track from town. A dark shape moving rapidly soon became an ominous van bumping towards the village. Slowing down briefly near the Chief's house, it then careered over the ruts before coming to a screeching halt by the church. A white officer stepped down from the front as a cluster of black police in uniform burst out from the doors at the back. The doors slammed shut and the van then hurtled off up the track towards the western slope and the far end of Bophelong. It was the direction of the Dikobe house. As it went out of sight over the top of the rise, Naledi felt sick.

One of the men disgorged from the van raised a large metal horn to his mouth:

> "No one is to leave the village. We are here to find the terrorist who burnt your Chief's house. You must all stay in your homes until we say you can go. Anyone trying to leave will be shot!"

Policemen darted off in different directions, their rifles

forward, while the white officer spoke into a radio which he held close to his face.

The queue at the tap froze. A tall, square-shouldered man stalked up to them, waving his arm.

"You heard! Hurry up! Go home!"

People wavered. They needed the day's water. Could they not get their water first? They looked uncertainly at the policeman. A couple of small terrified children ran away from the line crying, their empty cans swinging and knocking their legs. With a brief nod, the policeman indicated that the rest could collect their water, but with his finger signed only one bucket each. Naledi could feel the tension in Tiro's body as they got closer to him. She herself felt cold and stiff beside this great block of a man with a gun. Yet it was also so ridiculous! Something between a scream and a laugh seemed to jam in her throat. Who could be so dangerous about a water queue?

The other policemen were spreading out between the houses, shouting the order to stay indoors. The man with the horn continued to blare out his message further up the village while the white police officer seemed to keep scanning the distance along the track from the town.

Hurrying home with a barely half-filled bucket each, Naledi and Tiro caught sight of a great khaki truck approaching the village but still some distance away. It slowed down and a couple of figures jumped off. Then it began to veer across the veld, stopping every now and again to let more figures out. They seemed to be making a ring around the village.

For the next few hours Naledi and Tiro were confined to the house, keeping watch from the window in the room where they slept and where Nono could not see them. To stop Dineo pestering in her high voice, "What can you see? I want to see!" they let her squeeze in between them and put their fingers to their lips, as if they were playing a secret game.

From time to time one of them would go and snatch a brief glance through the doorway or through the window next to Nono's bed. From there you could see up to the church. Nono seemed slightly better and although Naledi had told her about the fire and that there were police in the village, she did not want her grandmother to become more worried by showing anxiety herself. Besides, the place she was thinking about most was out of sight – Taolo's house. She and Tiro knew that the police van had been heading that way. In the distance they occasionally caught sight of figures whose clothes seemed to be almost the same colour as the veld. They were carrying guns and appeared to be patrolling the outskirts. It looked as if the police within the village were moving from house to house, starting with the outermost dwellings and coming inwards. That meant they would come to Nono's house towards the end. What would they want to know? Would they ask Naledi about Taolo? She would say nothing except that they were in school together. Nothing.

As the hours passed Naledi's stomach felt as if it were being wrung out like a piece of washing. It was almost unbearable not knowing what was happening. She busied herself by preparing a meal of pap and beans. Not allowed outside, she could not cook in the usual pots on an open fire in the yard so instead had to use up precious parrafin in the small burner Mma had brought them. If it had been a normal day she would be hungry. But today she went through the motions of cooking without a single tastebud reacting.

The food was almost ready when Tiro signalled to her to come into the side room.

'They're over there!" he whispered.

He pointed to the Sadires' house. Their yards almost ajoined. A policeman was jabbing his rifle into the small shed attached to the back wall. It would be their turn soon. At the same moment a piercing shout was followed by David Sadire, the older boy, stumbling out of the door at the front. His arms jerked inwards, grasping his sides. A policeman appeared close behind, his rifle at David's back forcing him into a trot in the direction of the church. What could David have done? He was so quiet and hard-working, certainly not outspoken like Taolo.

Naledi forced her own chilled limbs to move. Fortunately Dineo was tired of looking out of the window and was now playing on the floor with her doll Pula.

"Come here, Neo. We must sit with Nono now."

Tiro remained at the window but Naledi, led Dineo by the hand to the chair next to Nono's bed. The little girl clutched her doll tightly. Nono welcomed them with her eyes. Naledi, Dineo and Pula sat on the chair, waiting.

CHAPTER 11

"What do you know about the fire at the chief's house?"

"Are you friendly with the Dikobe people?"

"What do you discuss with Mma Tshadi?"

"Are you the one who's making trouble in school?"

"Why don't you answer?"

The man firing the questions at Naledi in a low, sure voice did not seem to be just an ordinary policeman, the sort who simply beat, chased and pushed people around. He was not carrying a rifle like the other man who was hurriedly scouring the house, searching under Nono's bed and through the cupboard and chest of drawers. Instead the black handle of a small gun protruded from a leather bag strapped to his waist. He knew a lot about the village, and he stared at Naledi intently as he asked each question. He would wait for a few seconds for an answer and then break the silence with another question. His manner was unnerving and Naledi avoided looking at him. Hugging Dineo close to her thigh, she concentrated her gaze on the plaited patterns in her sister's hair.

"Why don't you answer? If you won't talk to me I shall have to take you to my boss."

It was Nono who saved her.

"Why do you ask my granddaughter so many questions? Can't you see that I am sick? The child hasn't time for anything but her studies and looking after us all here. Young man, why don't you go and ask your questions to people who have time to roam the streets?"

Nono's voice was not angry, simply calm and reasonable. Where did she get this sudden strength from? Naledi stole a direct glance at the man's face. She saw deep furrows form along his light brown forehead and his eyes narrow behind a pair of thinly rimmed spectacles. For a second it seemed he might explode into anger. Then unexpectedly he smiled:

"You know, Mma, you remind me of my grandmother, always ready to defend the younger ones." He paused and the smile was gone. "But these aren't children's games I'm talking about now. These children today are getting mixed up in big matters they don't understand. It's dangerous. If we don't teach them to leave these things alone, they'll get hurt and many families will be crying."

"I know what you are speaking about, young man, and you are right that many families are crying. But I'm saying to you that this child of mine here doesn't have time for these things."

Naledi felt the policeman's eyes shift back to her and the tone in which he spoke was once again sharp:

"You are lucky to have such a good grandmother. You'd be stupid to get mixed up with this politics business because you will only hurt yourself and your family. Terrorists get help in villages like this one. They start with setting fire to a chief's house, next thing it's a police-station. But we have already found some trouble-makers here and they will soon be happy to tell us what they know. You see, we find out everything in the end, so I'm giving you a warning. If I have questions to ask you another time, I will make sure you answer them."

He turned briskly towards the door, nodding towards the man with the rifle to follow.

"Good-bye Mma," he said grimly, without waiting for Nono to reply.

As soon as he had gone, Naledi clasped her grandmother's hand.

"If you hadn't spoken, Nono, he would have taken me! How can they be so cruel? What do they want with David Sadire? They surely have Taolo! What evidence have they got? They are just trying to frighten us!"

Nono patted Naledi's hand.

"My child, the policeman was right that these things are dangerous and bring many tears. It's better to leave them alone. I pray to God that He will change the hearts of those who are so hard to poor people like us."

"Nono, what they are doing to us, it's wrong, it's wicked! How can we sit and do nothing?"

Nono did not reply but Naledi felt a great sigh inside her grandmother's body. Nono let her head drop over onto the pillow, painfully turning her body to face the wall. Naledi leaned over her:

"I won't do anything silly, Nono, don't worry!"

When Nono still did not speak, Naledi began to straighten the sheet and blankets, rapidly wiping her hand across her face to stop Dineo from seeing the tears in her eyes. Dineo had been watching everything with wide, serious eyes. One set of fingers clutched an ear while the thumb of the other was stuck tightly in her mouth. Pula lay on the floor where she had been dropped when the police had entered.

Tiro, who had been standing stiffly by the entrance to the small side room all the time, now broke the silence.

"I hate them!" he hissed.

*

The moment the police van began bumping its way out of the village, doors opened wide and details of the raid passed rapidly over the yards and across the veld to and from the outermost dwellings. The ring of soldiers around the village, had been ordered back into the truck. The soldiers had not actually done anything except look menacing but they had threatened to shoot anyone trying to leave.

Naledi and Tiro hurried out with buckets for the tap. Stopping first at the Sadire house, they found David's four younger brothers and sisters huddled inside. Their mother had left early in the morning for work in the town, before the police had arrived. The eldest girl, about Tiro's age, said the policeman with glasses had shouted at David that they would find out everything about the fire. David had protested that he knew nothing about it until that morning but the policeman had hit him on the mouth, saying, "We are not fooled by liars!"

Then they had taken David away, pulling him by the hair and poking him with a rifle.

"What will they do to him? Our brother is not a liar!"

Naledi wanted to reassure the children, but what was there to say? Their mother would not return until later in the evening. In the meantime Naledi told them to wait in their grandfather's house. She watched as they straggled disconsolately up the track, the elder girl humping the baby on her back.

The news was discussed at the bulging, busy water queue. People said Mma Tshadi had been taken away. Was she a suspect just because she had argued with the chief? Others had seen both Saul Dikobe and his son being forced into the van. Hearing the news second-hand was too much for Naledi to bear. Leaving her bucket with Tiro, she dashed off to the Dikobe house. Out of breath, she found Mma Dikobe packing a small bag. Her face looked strained:

"I intended calling by to see your grandmother before leaving for Jo'burg. You've heard about Saul and Taolo? I want to notify Saul's lawyer immediately and see what can be done. I'm relieved they didn't take you too. It seems they're clutching at straws and that can be dangerous."

"What do you mean, Mma?"

"It means they take anyone and beat them up until they get the answers they want."

Naledi bit her lip as she watched Mma Dikobe pick up a comb from the table and put it into her bag before clicking the lock.

Walking back through the village with Mma Dikobe, Naledi felt a kind of pride fighting with her fears. Whatever the policeman had threatened, she could not help admiring Mma Dikobe and she was glad to be walking beside her. The policeman said they would find out everything, but what was wrong in being friends with the Dikobe family? Yet the police were so powerful.

When they reached the house, Mma Dikobe sat down next to Nono, talking calmly as if her only concern was how the old lady was feeling and getting on. Nono asked about the small suitcase and told her not to delay herself but Mma Dikobe insisted on making a thorough check. At last she declared herself satisfied that the pills were taking effect and that, with plenty of rest, Nono should continue to improve. As she was counting out more tablets onto the table, Mma Kau arrived. Dark shadows scored the skin beneath her eyes and she did not seem to have her usual easy manner. Pulling out a stool for her, Naledi could not stop herself from coming straight to the point.

"Did the police also trouble you, Mma? Is your son all right?"

Mma Kau looked vague: "He . . . he wasn't here when the police came. Last night he told me he had to go back to work right away."

"But Mma he only just came home."

Mma Dikobe put her hand on Naledi's shoulder:

"Can you make some tea, Naledi? I'm sure the police have already exhausted Mma Kau with questions."

While they drank the tea, Mma Kau hardly spoke. She sat upright with her head bowed slightly forward and her hands in her lap. Mma Dikobe had to remind her about the tea. Nor did she seem really aware of Dineo when she came to greet her. To Naledi the change in Mma Kau was startling. Yesterday she had been so strong and sure, helping out their family. Today Mma Kau herself was in need of help. Something must have happened to her son. Why had he left so suddenly? Naledi remembered his silent face under the checked cap as he stood at the back of the crowd outside the Chief's house the previous afternoon, and in that instant she knew what must be in Mma Kau's mind. It was something that could not be discussed. Glancing from Mma Dikobe to Nono, Naledi felt they knew too.

Mma Dikobe left late in the afternoon, saying that if she missed the last train to Jo'burg she would spend the night with a nursing friend in Boomdal and travel early the next morning. She was not sure when she would return.

CHAPTER 12

Dear Mma,

Sitting at the table in the lamplight, Naledi struggled to finish a letter to her mother, far away in Jo'burg:

"I don't know what will happen about the move, Mma. Most people say we should refuse to go. But we don't even know when they will send the trucks. I know it's hard for you to leave your work so I will just have to write to let you know what is happening. We all think about you."

Naledi chewed on her thumb. There was so much more she wanted to tell her mother, so much she had left out. She had not mentioned school, nor her contact with the Dikobes. It was not just that she did not want to add to Mma's worries. From her friend Grace she had learnt to be careful about putting things on paper. When replying to Naledi the first time, Grace had casually referred to some letters being read out in a court case against two young people who had been corresponding. Naledi had got the message; letters could be opened by the police. They could be sent on after their contents had been read and copied and you might not even know. Yet however careful Grace had been, perhaps she too was now missing – Naledi had still not had a reply to her last letter.

The following day Mma Tshadi returned on foot alone. She and the Dikobes and David Sadire had been kept overnight in the local police cells in Boomdal. She had been locked up in the women's section until early in the morning when a white man, not in police uniform, had spoken to her briefly before ordering her release. No explanation had been given and she had no further news about the others.

In the days that followed, Naledi's mind was often

far away, imagining what might be happening to Taolo, his father and to David Sadire in some police station somewhere. Were they still being kept at the police post in Boomdal or had they been taken further away for questioning? Tales of what happened inside such places were like nightmares.

Returning to school the day after the raid, Naledi prepared to say a meaningless, "I'm sorry", to Mr Molaba. The raid had helped make up her mind. There seemed no point in defying him on her own right now. She would only get expelled and it would not change anything. It would stop her from meeting other students. School was the only place where they had any chance of getting together to discuss things, in spite of the headmaster trying to stop them. But Mr Molaba did not even call her to his office. Had he forgotten? Or was he leaving her alone for a purpose? What if he had asked one of the students to spy on her? She would have to be careful.

Something, however, had changed at school. On the surface the students still seemed to be knuckling under Molaba's iron rule but remarks were being made under their breath, looks were being exchanged and heels silently but impatiently tapped during assembly. There was a new suppressed mood of agitation. Everyone seemed to know about the raid on Bophelong and the arrests. Taolo's name was mentioned in whispers.

At break-time Mr Molaba patrolled the school yard, making it impossible for any group of students to get together for serious discussions. Miriam joined Naledi beside the wire fence. Naledi was talking in a low voice when quite unexpectedly, two of the older students who had been present at Naledi's beating approached them, one of them calling out boldly with a grin:

"Why do you look out in the road when you've got handsome fellows like us inside here?!"

"Tlang kwano . . . come on! At least you can talk to us!" joked the other.

"Maybe they're shy because we never told them our names!" laughed the first.

"No problem! He's Zach and I'm Dan!"

The faces of the two girls must have shown their bafflement until the first boy whispered rapidly, "Make like you're joking. The hyena's watching."

A sideways glance told Naledi that Mr Molaba was looking across at them. In between loud chatter the boys interjected their message: some of the top class students were aiming to get the head's permission to hold a Students' Christian prayer meeting. They knew a sympathetic priest who would lead it and they would then arrange for Mr Molaba to be called away at the same time. If they secretly banged a nail into one of his car tyres, he would want it repaired at once as he always liked to leave school promptly. Even if he took a couple of students to help him change the wheel, the rest could be in the prayer meeting, and in between the hymns, they could discuss plans to resist the removal.

"Tell all your friends to attend the prayer meeting," Dan whispered.

"Why won't your granny let me visit you? I've got good manners!" Zach burst out with a peal of laughter.

"Get lost! What makes you think I even want you to visit," Naledi retorted. Her eyes carried another message. Taking Miriam by the arm, she walked off.

To Naledi's surprise Mr Molaba agreed at once to the prayer meeting. She had thought he might see through the idea but it appeared he was pleased that some of his students were showing an interest in religion. Nor did he suspect anything when they asked if Rev Radebe could lead the meeting. Rev Radebe was well known as a popular priest in the community and perhaps the headmaster thought the students had asked for him because he led one of the largest congregations in Boomdal as well as sometimes taking services at the church in Bophelong. When Rev Radebe was elected as one of the people's representatives on the Boomdal Resistance Committee that week-end, it was too late for Mr Molaba to change his mind without looking foolish. After all, the students had only asked for the priest to lead them in prayers.

As the day of the meeting drew near it became clear that so many students wanted to attend that a classroom would be too small. Mr Molaba agreed that it could be held in the front yard. Fortunately his car was always parked at the back of the school so if he could only be kept busy there he would be out of the way.

On the day, Rev Radebe arrived as the bell rang for break. Students poured down the steps from their classrooms. Naledi slipped her pen into the pocket of her blouse. A message had been passed around that everyone should bring a pen or pencil as well as their hymn books. She looked across the yard at the priest as he got out of his ageing blue Ford, smiling. Was he really going to help them have a meeting, right here in the lion's den? He seemed so relaxed and jovial as he strode in his long black cassock towards Mr Molaba, his hand outstretched. They were certainly a contrast, the large headmaster with his closely trimmed hair, small unfriendly eyes and facial skin stretched tightly across his cheeks, and the short priest with his bush of hair, plumpish cheeks and lively eyes. Together they walked up the steps to where Mr Molaba usually stood towering above them at assembly. All chatter stopped as the headmaster surveyed them. Naledi who was close to the front watched him finger the lapels of his jacket. Then he drew himself up to his full height, narrowed his eyes and after an inward breath said: "I am pleased to welcome Rev Radebe here today and I am happy to see that so many children in my school wish to spend this break-time in prayer. As you know I have been worried that some of you might be led into foolishness and so destroy yourselves. It relieves me to see you have not forgotten God who will teach you the path of patience. That said, I will now hand you over to Rev Radebe."

"Thank you, headmaster. I, too, was delighted when your students approached me with this idea of a prayer meeting. These are difficult times and God is there to give us strength if only we call on him. So let us begin today by singing one of my favourite hymns *Onward Christian Soldiers.*"

Hymn books were opened and pages turned when two students came hurrying from behind the classroom block. Instead of joining the assembly they approached the steps. Mr Molaba looked sternly towards them. One of the boys spoke in a low but clear whisper.

"Excuse us, sir. We were just coming from the toilets and we noticed your car has a flat tyre at the front."

The headmaster's gaze pierced the two boys for a second before he nodded his head in irritation. He turned to Rev Radebe, "Will you excuse me? I had better go and look at this right away."

He signalled to the students who had brought the news.

"Come with me."

Together they disappeared around the corner of the building as a host of voices rose into the air:

"Onward Christian Soldiers marching as to war."

Rev Radebe's theme was courage. In between hymns he spoke about Moses and the Jews maintaining their faith while slaves in the mighty state of Egypt; of Daniel thrown to the lions because of his refusal to deny his faith and submit to the powerful state of Babylon; about the early Christians in the very jaws of the Roman state; about saints and martyrs who had suffered death rather than deny what they believed to be right.

"It is in your heart of hearts that God plants his message. You must listen very carefully to it."

He made no direct references, but Naledi felt as if her mind were in flames. He was talking about their own situation. He was encouraging them to do what they themselves believed was right, to follow the path of courage and take the consequences.

"What I'm saying to you is not easy. There are also other important qualities that we need besides courage. Now, I'm not going to tell you them. This is where your pens come in. I've asked some of my young friends to give out some blank paper and I want each of you to write down the five qualities you think are most important for any human being. I like to know what young people are thinking. Please don't discuss the matter at this point with your neighbour. Just think about it yourself very quietly. You will have three minutes and then hand your papers in."

Pieces of paper were rapidly passed along the lines but they weren't blank. Handing the bundle on to her neighbour, Naledi looked at the paper. Printed down the side were the numbers one to five and at the top, in capital letters, were the words:

> THIS IS YOUR CHANCE TO ELECT THE STUDENTS YOU WANT TO REPRESENT YOU IN OUR STRUGGLE AGAINST REMOVAL. WRITE THE NAMES OF FIVE STUDENTS.

So this was what it was all about! A meeting to elect representatives! A low murmur rippled through the students which Rev. Radebe calmed with a hand signal. Did he know the papers were not blank or had the organisers replaced the papers without his knowledge? Whoever was involved certainly had courage.

Naledi wrote down five names, starting with Taolo Dikobe. Just because he was expelled and the police had got him at the moment should not stop him being a representative. She hoped others would think the same way. As the papers were being collected in Mr Molaba came back. Rev Radebe was quick to explain his request to the students.

"I can let you know the outcome of my little survey if you wish," he added.

"Thank you," replied Mr Molaba with a hint of curtness in his voice as he held his greasy hands rather awkwardly away from his jacket. The slight twitching of his forehead suggested he was holding irritation in check while Rev Radebe recited a final prayer. Naledi exchanged secret smiles with her neighbours. It was not often that you could see Mr Molaba ill at ease, she thought as she mouthed 'Amen'. What would be his expression if he knew what was in the bundle of papers?

CHAPTER 13

From the moment Zach called Naledi aside in the school yard the following day to say she had been elected onto the student committee, something changed in her. There was no longer time simply to sit and wonder what was happening to Taolo in jail, or what was going to happen to them all. News of who had been elected spread rapidly through the school and before she had time even to think about what it would mean to be a student representative people were coming to her with their complaints and suggestions. If Mr Molaba was observing the yard he would surely sense something was up, but there was no time even to worry about that.

Naledi's election took her by surprise. It must be, she supposed, because of the beating and the connection with Taolo. There had been an overwhelming vote for him in spite of his expulsion and detention by the police. Zach and Dan had both been elected as well as a girl called Theresa from the top class. There were at least five more popular names to form a pool so that if anyone were arrested, someone else could step in. A boy in Naledi's class, Ben Mosai, would work in Taolo's place until he was released from prison. The first meeting of the student committee was arranged for the next day straight after school at Zach's house which was close to the school. His mother and the neighbours would be out at work. Since any meetings required permission from the authorities, they would have to be careful.

Although Naledi and Theresa hardly knew each other, Theresa suggested they link arms to look relaxed as they made their way to Zach's house. Any inquisitive person would just think they were Zach's latest girl-friends. It was not difficult to play the part, as Theresa bubbled over with funny remarks about Mr Molaba and other members of their school. The others slipped into the small main room one by one and sat down at the cramped kitchen table. There was only one other room to the left with hardly space to walk between the table and a bed along the wall. On the right side a curtain pulled across the room suggested it had been partitioned to give someone privacy. Zach saw Naledi looking at the curtain and explained:

"My older sister and her husband live with us but they don't come back until late."

Then giving his younger brother and sister a couple of cents each, Zach asked them to play outside and keep watch for him. Pocketing the money with wide smiles, they nodded and ran outside.

Zach was businesslike:

"It's not safe to be here more than half an hour so we must work quickly. This is our first student committee meeting and we want everyone in Boomdal to see what we can do when we stick together. We could start with a march from school to Boomdal Council Offices and from there to the white people's Town Hall. Dan and I have been speaking to students and nearly all of them want to show openly that they are against this removal. It's time we stopped being pushed around."

Dan explained that the route of the march would go past the primary school so those children could also join in. It would be peaceful, with students only carrying posters and placards.

"Those Boomdal councillors will call the police. What shall we do then?" asked Theresa.

"We keep going. We can't let them frighten us any more."

"That's what Molaba does to us all the time."

"We'll only be marching. We're not threatening."

"Everybody must see what we think about this removal. Our parents and the old people must know that we're determined not to move. There's no other way."

It was decided that immediately after assembly on the following Monday, instead of marching into class, the students would all turn around and march out of the school. Zach's elder brother had a van which could be parked outside the gates and in which the placards could be hidden. Mr Molaba could shout as much as he liked, but they would all ignore him and begin their march. The message about the Monday march would not give the exact time so that if the teachers heard about it, they would not be able to make precise plans to stop it.

Each of the five agreed on what was to be done before Monday. Naledi's main task was to inform students from the first class in their school and to make contact with the primary school. They would aim to march past during the morning break. Tiro and Zach's brother and sister could warn a few children whom they trusted to encourage others to join the marchers. They would not spread the news around too widely at first in case the younger children told their parents who might order them not to join in or perhaps even stop them from going to school that day. Finally it was agreed that Zach and Dan would ask the Boomdal Resistance Committee if they wanted student representatives.

Within half an hour, the meeting was over. Naledi and Theresa left, first calling good-bye to the two young look-outs with a show of chatting and laughing. They parted outside the general dealer's store, giving each others' hands a quick squeeze.

Walking quickly, sometimes jogging, along the track back to Bophelong, Naledi was not sure whether she felt more excited or nervous. She had never been involved in anything as big as this before. To her Soweto friend Grace and to Taolo, protest marches were nothing new. But however much she had heard about them, actually helping to organise and take part in one herself was like stepping into the unknown. Was it the same for the others too? What still surprised her was the dramatic change in Zach and Dan. Although she had hardly known them before this, at her beating they had stood silently by, following Mr Molaba's instructions. Yet afterwards there had been that look of shame in their eyes. Had something then snapped in both of them to lead them to what they were doing now? They were all on a collision course with authority.

Naledi had told Nono that she would be a little late because she had to help Mr Gwala to clear up. She hated lying to her grandmother but it would have been impossible to tell the truth without causing yet more worry. Hadn't she already promised Nono she would not do anything stupid? And what she was doing now wasn't at all stupid. In fact, it was the only sensible thing to do – but she knew Nono would not see it that way. However much her grandmother complained, in the end, she would always say you had to do what the government said because they could easily kill you without it bothering them at all.

Naledi found Nono out of bed and in the yard, bending over a cooking pot. She felt a pang of guilt. Was it because she was late?

"You shouldn't be up Nono. You still need to rest. Let me do that," she said moving forward to take the large wooden spoon.

But her grandmother shuffled her aside.

"When a teacher needs help that is more important. I can manage."

Did Nono mean that, or was she upset that Naledi was late? She did not look at her grand-daughter so Naledi could not tell from her expression.

"Please Nono, let me do it now."

"No, it's finished. Go and find Dineo. Your brother fetched her from Mma Kau but now she's playing somewhere. Tell them to come and eat."

Naledi found her brother and sister with a group of children in the veld behind the houses. Tiro was sitting to one side of a broken tree stump while the little ones played a game of chase and catch. Dineo was jumping up and down, swirling and shivering with excitement, joining in the shouting as each new person was caught and turned chaser. Tiro looked up at Naledi as she approached. It seemed he had stopped smiling since this removal business had begun.

"Nono wants us," Naledi called.

Dineo came racing over, laughing and twisting past Naledi's outstretched arm.

"Can I play some more?" she begged.

Naledi shook her head: "Tomorrow."

Walking back to the house with Dineo dancing ahead, Naledi spoke quietly to Tiro about the plans for the march, explaining how they were to be kept secret in case teachers and parents tried to stop it. Tiro seemed confident that younger children as well as those from his class and the other higher would want to join in.

"Do you think they'll shoot?" Tiro asked.

Naledi did not reply. It was something she had not wanted to think about. She had been pushing back any dreadful pictures in her mind of shootings. She knew it had happened in other places but if they began to let those thoughts frighten them, they would never make any protest at all but just give in to everything. They weren't planning to be violent, only to carry posters. Was it right, though, to let the younger primary children come? Yet having started the march, how could they stop them joining in? When the government sent its trucks to move them, everyone would be thrown onto them, little children too. They were all caught up in something much bigger than themselves. No-one was safe and there was no escape. Why couldn't all the adults see this? Nono would say you might as well give in, for the sake of peace. But where was peace?

Naledi was jerked back to the present as Tiro said bitterly, "We should have guns like them."

CHAPTER 14

Over the weekend Naledi couldn't stop Nono working around the house and yard. She even spoke of returning to work on the white farm and would not listen to Naledi's protests.

"What do you know about these things?" she said curtly.

Nono was worried that in the two weeks she had been away someone else might have been taken on in her place. But it seemed to Naledi that something else was bothering her grandmother. Had she suspicions about the students' plans? Was she angry because she thought Naledi was going to involve the family in further trouble? There was no way of finding out without giving away too much.

On the Sunday Nono insisted she was well enough to go to church.

"We must pray to God to help us now," she said. Many villagers, as well as workers residing on white-owned farms in the surrounding district, regularly attended the church on Sundays. It was a chance to share anxieties and exchange the week's news. From Nono's conversations with other older people, Naledi sensed an air of grim determination mixed with despair. Rra Rampou told Nono.

"They can kill me first. They won't take me alive from here."

Mma Tshadi alone showed no trace of defeat.

"Yes, we shall pray, Mma Modibe," she said to Nono resolutely, "but praying by itself is not enough. When an ox gets his foot stuck in a hole, does he just stand there? No Mma, he tries to pull it out and he makes us all hear his roar so we will come to help him. Can we not also roar so others will come to help us?"

Nono nodded faintly. She would not openly contradict Mma Tshadi when she spoke with such conviction.

Supporting her grandmother up the worn steps of the old stone church's narrow doorway. Naledi glanced past the deserted tap and along the track up to the west. Rra Thopi's house was visible above the sloping veld, but that was not what caught her eye. It was a familiar figure half-way down the path, walking in their direction.

"Mma Dikobe's back, Nono!"

Naledi was so excited she wished she could run straight off to speak to her. But she could not leave Nono. She waved, not sure whether she was seen. Even Nono turned, smiling slightly, before continuing on her unsteady feet towards the benches.

Mma Dikobe found a seat behind them, barely having

time to exchange greetings before the priest arrived. To Naledi's disappointment it was not Rev Radebe. Concentrating on the sermon was impossible when all she wanted to know was whether Mma Dikobe had brought news of Taolo and his father. When the service was over, Mma Dikobe came to take Nono's arm.

"How is it with you Mma? Shouldn't you still be resting?" she asked with concern.

As the congregation edged its way out of the shaded building into the bright sunshine of the yard, other villagers greeted Mma Dikobe. People who had previously been withdrawn and suspicious of the Dikobe family now showed obvious pleasure at her return. It was Mma Tshadi who asked directly:

"What news do you bring of your husband and your son, Mma?"

Mma Dikobe looked down as she answered, perhaps hiding the pain in her eyes:

"The only news I have is that they are in Modderbee Prison. It took a whole week just to find out that. Saul's lawyer tried to get permission to see him but they won't let him in."

She herself had been to the prison and to the police headquarters in Johannesburg. All she had been told was that there were no charges yet against the two of them, but they were being held under the Terrorism Act and could be detained for as long as the police wanted. It was not only the burning of Chief Sekete's house that was being investigated. According to the lawyer, there had been other incidents in neighbouring areas, including the petrol-bombing of a police station, and the police were trying to find a link.

When Mma Dikobe finished speaking, Mma Tshadi took her free hand;

"You are part of our family now Mma. It was very wrong for us to treat you like unwelcome strangers. We believed all the stories our chief made up. But now we can see with our own eyes how he has run away and how you have been helping us. Yesterday I sent two of my children to give your plants water. They were growing so nicely before you left. The children will come and help you carry water and firewood and also do weeding if you wish. It's not easy to be on your own."

Mma Tshadi's apology was supported by remarks and gestures from all the surrounding women, including Nono who patted Mma Dikobe's arm. For the first time Naledi saw tears welling up in Mma Dikobe's eyes. Withdrawing her hand from Mma Tshadi's firm clasp, she lightly wiped the corners of her eyes.

"I was without my husband for a long time. It's harder now because my son is gone as well. They've taken so many children. But we shall manage. We won't let them crush us so easily."

Although she said the last words softly, her voice trembled with an unspoken anger. Then she added:

"If your children come, I'll be glad to see them, thank you Mma." Excusing herself from the small gathering, Mma Dikobe helped Nono across the church yard.

"Let me bring you home Mma. I want to check your pills," she said.

*

Naledi found it hard to fall asleep that night. She was still thinking about the march long after Nono and Dineo had settled down to sleep in the adjoining room. Even Tiro had stopped shifting restlessly on the mat next to her. Would they get safely back the following night? Even if they returned unhurt, she felt she would come back in some way different, changed. On that march tomorrow they would be taking steps that could never be undone. Did Nono sense this? In the church yard Naledi had noticed her grandmother listening intently to all the conversations. Although Nono did not refer to it, somehow Naledi felt that if she ever needed an ally who could explain to her grandmother that she was not being 'stupid', Mma Dikobe was that person. As she lay listening to the night's deep silence, it was unexpectedly broken by soft pattering on the thatch above. With the rains beginning, perhaps it would be a good year for the crops after all, if they were still there to reap them. The sense of being warm under her blanket while outside the earth was being refreshed soothed Naledi and finally lulled her to sleep.

*

Usually Tiro set off well before Naledi but on this Monday morning, after collecting the water, Naledi prepared to leave with him. Nono noticed but said nothing, watching Naledi from her bed. Mma Dikobe had managed to persuade her not to return to work for at least another week, promising to write a letter to the farmer, if possible on hospital notepaper. With luck the job would be kept for her.

If Nono asked why she was leaving so early, Naledi had again planned to say that Mr Gwala required some extra help, this time in the school garden. She felt very unsure, though, whether Nono would really believe her and so it was a relief not to be questioned. But she felt guilty about Nono, and even more so when, as they said good-bye, there was a look in her grandmother's eyes which was not angry but immeasurably sad.

CHAPTER 15

The air was crisp in the early morning chill with the smell of dampness arising from the earth as Naledi and

Tiro joined a group of children on their way to school. Some jogged and wrapped their arms around themselves in an attempt to warm up beneath their thin clothes.

"Has your headmaster sent you back to primary school?" one of the children joked to Naledi.

"Don't be stupid! She's a student representative now!" Tiro butted in almost fiercely. "There's a big march today. They'll come right past our school so we can join it."

The questions flooded out. Where? When? Why weren't they told earlier? Naledi explained, making it clear that the teachers should not be told in case they then forced their pupils to stay indoors.

"I'll beat up anyone who tells!" breathed a boy slightly smaller than Tiro. He flexed his arms, shooting sharp punches into the air, shaking all the folds in his oversized coat.

As they hurried across the veld in anticipation of the march, they passed one of the village boys who did not go to school. He was wielding a long stick behind a jostling herd of cattle. His two dogs rushed barking and yapping through the grass towards the school group.

"Why such a hurry today?" he called.

"Tell you later!" the boy in the coat shouted back.

The herd-boy whistled, his dogs racing back to him.

The five high-school representatives met behind the general store, to avoid suspicion by being at school too early. Naledi was the first to arrive. Waiting gave her time to think and she suddenly felt very nervous. This action they were about to take was full of complications and uncertainties. If something happened to her and Tiro, how would Nono cope? That look of sadness in Nono's eyes haunted her. Should she have chosen to stay out of all this? But how, when the removal was being forced on them?

Expecting the shop-keeper to come out through the back door at any moment and chase her away, she watched the faces of passers-by along the nearby road. What if the others had also had second thoughts about the march and were backing out? Only when she saw Zach and Dan's lanky figures overtake a woman balancing a bulky case on her head, did her doubts recede. She was no longer alone. With the arrival of Theresa and Ben shortly afterwards they were complete – and ready for action.

Zach and Dan had already prepared and stacked posters in the van which Zach's brother would park outside the school just before assembly time. Both would stand at the back of their class lines, nearest the gates, to lead the students out and hand them placards as they passed. The signal would be when Mr Molaba intoned his usual "Good-morning children". That would be the moment for them to shout "We march," and begin the exodus. They would immediately start the chant, "We won't move, we won't move," to drown out whatever Mr Molaba and the teachers might try to shout.

In the school yard the excitement was almost tangible. Students were on edge, knowing the march was going to take place although not knowing the exact time. Surely Mr Molaba would suspect something.

After registration, they filed into the yard for assembly with Mr Molaba straight and alert, his eyes darting over the lines of students. Suddenly he called to Mr Gwala and, pulling a bunch of keys from his pocket, he pushed them into the teacher's hand while whispering an instruction. Mr Gwala began walking somewhat slowly towards the school gates. Was he going to lock them? There was no time to lose. Naledi was not sure who shouted first, but within seconds the cries, "We march," and, "We won't move," resounded upwards as the neat lines of students merged suddenly into a mass of bodies making for the gates.

"Run, Gwala!"

The headmaster bellowed with a great bull-like roar, but his voice was soon drowned. Pushed along in the rush for the gates, Naledi caught a brief glimpse of her teacher. He was not running. Instead he was standing well back from the headlong crowd, the keys to the gate dangling from one hand while he was shouting something himself, something like, "Slow down!". There was a danger people would be crushed going through the gates all at once. Then two boys leapt out of the main body and hurled themselves upwards onto the high fence. Fingers and arms grasped the wire, muscles tensed and heaved, as they pulled themselves over the top. Students cheered and others followed their lead. Naledi found herself being tightly wedged through the gate, then released on the other side. Glancing back, she saw the top of the fence beginning to sway with the weight of climbers but there was no time to watch. She had to encourage students to form themselves into lines. Zach and Dan were already further down the road running towards an old green van with its back doors swung open. As the students swarmed by, placards rapidly began to circulate among them, and were lifted up high.

NO REMOVALS! WE WON'T GO!
STOP CANING! RELEASE TAOLO DIKOBE!
WE SAY NO TO BOP! LEAVE US IN PEACE!
APARTHEID MUST GO – NOT US!

Women busy with laundry slowly straightened their backs, wiping soap-sud hands on aprons as they watched the students pass; elderly men raised bent heads; hens ran squawking along the ruts in the road seeking refuge through holes in fences; dogs barked and small children ran excitedly beside them, copying the chants; the owner of the general store came outside with his customers onto the raised verandah to investigate; a group of out-of-work young men stopped their game of cards to stare and shout comments. Everyone was taking notice!

The students grew more confident. Songs begun by those at the front spread along the entire length of the thick column of a few hundred students. All of Boomdal could surely hear them! Certainly the children at the primary school should have received advance warning. It was only around the next corner and then on to the Council offices. Perhaps the Councillors could even hear them coming!

Turning the corner Naledi saw primary children already running down the road to join them. A great cheer of greetings rose up from the secondary students. Seconds later excitement turned to terror. At the far end of the road in the hot, hazy distance the road was blocked. It seemed to be tightly packed with figures in uniform and it was just possible to make out dogs in front of them, straining at leashes.

A tense warning message was passed back through the crowd as more children continued to scramble over the locked gate and fence of the primary school, unaware of the danger from the other direction. Shouts produced puzzled looks, followed by confusion, when the primary children finally realised the danger. A few retreated, leaving some simply rooted to the spot and undecided. Others, ignoring the warnings, slipped in with the moving crowd. Naledi could not see Tiro but felt certain he would be marching forward. If she were next to him she could at least try to protect and restrain him if necessary. His hatred against all the injustice had been growing so deep that he was likely to be reckless. Trying to look behind her, she tripped, but luckily someone grabbed her arm. The pace of marching had quickened. The chant had returned to, "We don't move," and the whole student body was practically jogging to its rhythm. It was a call of defiance.

They were close enough to see that apart from the

men with dogs, many of the black police were carrying sjamboks, the dreaded stinging whips. A few white policemen were scattered among yet more black policemen in between vans parked on the open veld to the left. Here sjamboks were replaced by rifles. What should they do? The Council offices were off a road further on to the right. Their pace slowing, they continued forward until Zach's voice was heard calling for a halt. Only a couple of hundred metres now lay between them and the police. Someone shouted,

"This is a peaceful march! Let us through!"

The cry was taken up by voices all around. Could a couple of representatives not talk to the police, explain it was only a peaceful demonstration? Naledi began to squeeze her way through to the front when, without warning, a harsh shout from the police ranks was followed by viciously growling dogs suddenly bounding towards them. Their handlers came racing behind, yelling commands. As the dogs reached their targets, pulling down their first victims, policemen with raised sjamboks rushed at full pitch into the mass of screaming students. Sjamboks slashed into bodies, relentless, merciless. The only escape was onto the veld where the police lines were thinner.

Seeing a dog coming for her, Naledi pushed sideways as it leapt at her. It caught the hem of her dress. Desperate, she lunged through a gap between two police wielding sjamboks, giving her skirt a fierce tug. The thin material ripped. Protecting her head with her arms she bent down, edging rapidly through and over bodies. Crack! The whiplash of a sjambok across her shoulder and arms sent her stumbling down. A boot caught her in the ribs and she rolled over crumpled in pain, hands over her head. She was going to be crushed . . . until she felt hands under her armpits, lifting her, pulling her away. She tried to take some of her weight on her own legs, but a voice she recognised said, "Take it easy!"

It was student committee member Ben Modise helping her to get away. They were out of the main crush now but by no means safe from attack.

Students were bleeding, lying injured on the ground; others were still wrestling with police and dogs; some were being dragged into vans while others were running and throwing stones. The air crackled with the sound of shots. Naledi felt a chilling knot in her stomach: where was Tiro in all this devastation?

"It's okay . . . I'm all right," Naledi told Ben, letting go of his arm.

"It's not safe here. Come further!"

"No, I must find my brother," she insisted. Turning back again, she called Tiro's name over and over. It mingled with cries and screams. The main police attack was moving further down the road close to the primary school where children were now scaling the fence, trying to get back inside. Students were scattering over the veld, some running at full speed down the road they had come along. Others were disappearing into yards and houses.

Suddenly she saw Tiro on the veld opposite his school. She started to run to him. With a swift bending movement, he scooped up a stone and took aim. Naledi stopped in her tracks to follow the line of the shot. One of the dog-handlers jerked his hand up to his forehead. Blood ran down his face as he swung around. Identifying Tiro, he rushed at him, his dog stretched in full flight. Tiro raced in a wide curve, heading for the school fence, the dog almost at his heels. He leapt at the wire but he was not quite high enough. As his hands clutched the mesh, the dog snapped at his feet. With a monumental effort the boy pulled himself higher, kicking violently backwards to dislodge the animal. He slung himself over the top just as the policeman reached the fence. The gates which the teachers had locked to keep the children inside had also helped to keep the police out.

But not for long. A dense contingent of black policemen led by a white officer approached the school gates. A teacher in the yard who was calling children to hurry inside was summoned to the gates. Naledi watched anxiously to see what would happen. The police were after people like Tiro. She saw the teacher shake her head, then return to the building. A minute later the headteacher appeared. He walked in his dignified manner towards the police in spite of the shouts to hurry up. Naledi moved a little closer to hear the conversation. The police voices were becoming increasingly angry while the headmaster's voice remained soft and controlled. It was clear he did not want to let the police into his school. He was saying something about a warrant but the police threatened to cut the wire fence and to arrest him too. Reluctantly he produced a bunch of keys from his pocket and slowly opened the gates.

Two students joined Naledi, wanting to see who would be brought out. Although many of the police were now dispersed chasing and battling with students on the run, it would still be difficult to cope with the injured students who needed help. How could the badly injured be got to hospital? Their student committee had not planned for such things.

Zach came running up. It was urgent that they find houses where people would take in injured students before the police began to dump them into their trucks. There was no time to lose. News about Tiro would have to wait. The two students accompanied Naledi as she limped as quickly as she could in the direction of the houses. Many doors were shut, with residents either out at work or refusing to open up. They were probably scared. Some, however, readily agreed to take in the injured.

Soon students who could not walk were being carried indoors. Naledi's stomach turned at the sight of the injuries, deep long cuts from sjambok lashes, gashed and bitten flesh, skin pitted open with holes. She was shocked to find Theresa half-conscious with a gaping head wound. As she helped lift her friend, the pain of Naledi's own arms and shoulders seemed to lessen. She had got off lightly in the attack from this terrible enemy. How could people with eyes, ears and hearts do such things to other human beings? It was as if the students had been attacked not by humans but by one of those vast threshing and chopping machines which did not care where it struck, just like the bulldozers which the government would be sending to tear down their homes.

As the last of the injured were being brought in, Dan and some of the others set off to find transport to the hospital. It was possible that the police would raid the hospital but many of the wounds needed urgent attention. They would have to take the risk. Finding Zach, Naledi told him about her brother and he agreed that she should try to find him. Tiro's wound might also be serious and if the police got him, he might soon be in a much worse state. That policeman with the cut forehead would want his revenge.

Finding that the first session at the primary school was over, Naledi anxiously sought out children from her brother's class, but no one had seen him return to their classroom. Policemen had indeed come inside and examined them all, searching for a boy with a leg injury, but Tiro had not been there. What surprised them was that when their teacher was asked if anyone was missing, she had replied that everyone was present.

Was it possible that Tiro had managed to hide and escape? But where? Perhaps he had tried to get back home. With his injured foot, how far could he walk? Maybe he had collapsed along the way. She would have to follow the route he usually took. If only she could find him! The thought of having to tell Nono that Tiro was missing spurred on Naledi's aching body. Her eyes frantically scanned the roads, tracks and yards of

Boomdal and then the open veld as she jogged, limped, dragged and pushed herself along. She caught up and passed some of the straggling children with whom she and Tiro had travelled to school that morning. A few of them kept pace with her for a while but she hardly noticed them. The herdboy called a greeting and question which she did not answer. Instead she called to him.

"Did my brother pass here?"

When he shook his head, her whole body, hot and sticky with sweat, turned icy. Could Tiro have come the long way round? Surely not with his wound. It was also very unlikely that he would have gone to the hospital unless he was desperate.

Dineo was sitting in the yard pretending to feed her doll Pula when Naledi arrived. The child stared at her sister's torn dress and heaving body.

"Tiro? Is he here?" Naledi's voice throbbed.

The little girl shook her head as Nono's slow thin form appeared at the door. Her grandmother stood there perfectly still except for a slight twitch in the folds of wrinkled skin beneath remote, filmy eyes. Her hand clasped her mouth in a gesture of silence which Naledi did not know how to break. She had hurt Nono once before, taking Tiro off of Jo'burg without telling her. They had had to go then, to get Mma, or Dineo might have died. That time things had worked out. They had come back safely and Dineo had survived. This time things were not working out and she could not even tell Nono where Tiro was. She could only blurt out,

"We had to do it Nono! We had to!"

CHAPTER 16

Nono remained silent, not responding even to Dineo's whimpers. Naledi sat down, trying to quieten the child, cradling her on her lap. What could she say? She tried to explain to Nono what had happened, how the march was meant to be peaceful, how the police had started attacking them, how she had seen Tiro running away from them. She said nothing about the stone-throwing or about the dog biting him. That might just be too much for Nono.

At last when Dineo had quietened, Naledi was able to put her down and take out a needle and reel of black cotton from a little tin on the shelf. Removing her tunic, she carefully placed together the torn strips and began to stitch. Dineo watched, thumb in mouth. When she had finished mending her tunic, Naledi first asked, then begged, her grandmother to let her go back to Boomdal to search again for Tiro, but Nono's reply was an emphatic shaking of her head. The look in Nono's eyes, together with her silence, cut Naledi like a knife.

"Please Nono, please at least talk to me. If you blame me for Tiro, then let me go and look for him! I know you are worried the police will take me, but I promise I'll be careful. Tiro might be needing my help right now Nono!"

Naledi was unprepared for what followed. Nono's lower lip began to tremble and her breath came in uneven starts as she suddenly lifted her head towards her granddaughter, but it was as if she was gazing through her.

"Why did you not think about helping your brother before? What good is it now? Did you imagine the police would stand looking at all of you? You think someone as old as I am knows nothing, but you children are like chickens that want to fly behind netting."

The effort of speaking had been too much. Trying to

get up from her chair, Nono's hand shook as it gripped the table and she sank back into her seat. Naledi darted forward to support her, and lead her by gradual steps to the bed. Nothing more was said. Nono's condemnation was out in the open and it was worse than either the lash from the policeman's sjambok or from Mr Molaba's cane. Those just hurt her body but this hurt her heart. What was more, she could hate those people for their cruelty. But Nono's cutting words came out of her love and concern, and Naledi felt defenceless against her anger.

The tension and silence in the house were broken briefly in the early evening when Mma Kau called on her way back from visiting her sister in Boomdal. Her sister lived well beyond the council offices so they had not seen anything, but news of the police attack on the students had spread like wildfire. Children from a number of families were either injured or missing and there was an angry mood in Boomdal against the police. Mma Kau did most of the talking with Nono barely murmuring an occasional word. She tried to reassure Nono, reporting how people had been helping many children by letting them hide inside their houses. Tiro could still be hiding. But if he had not returned by the following morning, she promised to go herself to the hospital and to Boomdal police station.

Nono seemed to become a little calmer as she listened to Mma Kau, and her mention of the hospital gave Naledi an idea.

"Mma Dikobe may have seen Tiro if he went to the hospital! Let me go and ask her, please Nono! She should be home by now," Naledi pleaded.

"Let her go, Mma," put in Mma Kau sensing the tension. "She won't be away for long."

Glancing briefly at her grand-daughter, Nono consented.

But Mma Dikobe's house was dark and empty. Naledi

could see that as she approached it. Nevertheless she ran all the way up to the door and knocked. There was no reply. The light was fading rapidly and Mma Dikobe was usually home by this time. Had she perhaps switched to night work or had she stayed behind at the hospital to help with all the injured students? It was probably the second reason and Naledi once again felt torn between loyalties. She too should be in Boomdal helping those who had been hurt. She should be searching for her brother. Yet how could she leave her grandmother in her present condition.

She returned home, empty handed.

"It's still dark in her house," Naledi said quietly.

Mma Kau had gone and Nono barely looked up, as if expecting nothing. Dineo was asleep beside her on the bed. Remaining silent like a shadow from the candlelight, Nono signalled Naledi to sit and eat. After a meal in complete silence, Naledi prepared to sleep.

It was the first time she could remember the mat beside her being empty. Lying there curled up in her own corner she felt quite desolate and alone, even though Nono and Dineo were only on the other side of the open doorway. What hurt her so much was that look in Nono's eyes of distrust, accusing her of betrayal – as if she were the cause of Tiro being in trouble. Nono just did not understand. And what would their mother think? She knew nothing about this latest turn of events. Perhaps she also would not understand. She might say that Naledi as an older sister should have tried to stop Tiro becoming involved in the march. Mma would say he was too young. But it was not like that. If they all started worrying about protecting only themselves and their own family, they would never be able to change anything. How could they ever fight against an enemy which was like a great machine unless they all joined together? Even joined together they were still very weak, compared to an enemy which had so much power over them. They had so much to learn and a lot of them were going to be hurt. But whatever Mma and Nono thought, however much she loved them, Naledi knew that what she and the others had been doing was right. If they kept on giving in to this enemy injustice would go on forever.

Deep inside her, somewhere down in her stomach, Naledi felt a little ball harden as if it were tying up raw nerve endings. She would have to be hard if she was going to get through this thing. Tiro had been changing. If the police caught him now, she could not imagine him giving in to them. They would probably kill him first with their tortures. Dreadful images loomed up in her mind . . . of her brother struggling for breath as his sack-covered head was pushed into a bucket of water, of wires attached to his fingers and his skinny body jerking uncontrollably, of a lighted cigarette stubbed out on his skin, of his broken body splayed out on a cold prison floor.

Naledi fiercely bit her lower lip and deliberately switched her mind to Taolo, also in a prison cell. He seemed to have solid stone inside him. Yes, they would all have to become like rock, solid rock. Let the great machine smash itself against rock.

Naledi woke with a start as she heard soft knocking. Already Nono was shuffling off the bed next door.

"Wait Nono, I'll go," she called, lifting herself up and putting her hand to the wall as a guide. Feeling for the table in the main room she felt around for the candle and matches. With the room lit, she and Nono exchanged a brief anxious look, before she lifted the bolt. There, with Mma Dikobe's arm around his shoulders, was Tiro!

"We're very lucky to have this one back," said Mma Dikobe. Nono took Tiro into her arms. She held him close to her body as she leaned against the bed, one hand clasping his head. Only when he wriggled a little did she release him to look at him and give Naledi a chance to hug him too. Tossing on the bed, little Dineo pushed herself up, rubbing her eyes.

"What's wrong with your leg?" Nono asked, noticing him limp. Before he could reply, Mma Dikobe took Nono's arm and sat her down.

"Don't worry Mma. He's alright." Mma Dikobe's face was tired. Naledi made tea as they listened to what had happened to Tiro.

Tiro told how his teacher had seen the police coming after him as he ran back into the school, and had slipped him into the empty staffroom. In the corner was a large cupboard where she had hidden him beneath the shelves, locking the door and taking the key. Shortly afterwards he had heard heavy footsteps entering the staffroom, but no one had tried to open the cupboard. A voice said, "It's the teachers' room." Then they had left.

He had managed to take off his shirt and tie it around his foot, trying to stop the bleeding. Later teachers had come in for their break. Someone had tried to open the cupboard, complaining that he couldn't find the key to get a new exercise book. Tiro had heard his teacher interrupt, saying that she couldn't find the key either but she had a spare exercise book which the other teacher could use.

Locked in the cupboard until late in the afternoon, he had been aching with cramp and with the pain in his foot. His teacher had come to let him out only when everyone had gone home except for three friends from his class. She had asked them to stay behind to help her get him out of the school unnoticed. They had waited until the caretaker was attending to the toilets before bundling him out. Although Tiro had tried to walk normally, he felt so stiff and weak that if anyone had looked closely at the group they would have seen something was wrong. They helped him walk to the house of a friendly taxi-driver, then his friends left and his teacher took him to the hospital.

Mma Dikobe took over the story. The casualty clinic was flooded with injured students and she was called from her normal ward duties to help. In the middle of the afternoon police burst in demanding to see who was being treated. They hauled away a number of the older students for questioning, including one girl with a serious head wound whom they could see was hardly conscious. When a nurse tried to stop them pulling the girl from a bed, she was told to mind her own business or she too would be arrested. All protests from the hospital staff were ignored, including those of the white doctor in charge. It appeared the police were also looking for a younger child, a boy with a foot wound from a dog bite. The hospital was told to report any such case being brought to them.

But Mma Dikobe had seen Tiro in the waiting area and immediately took him over, attending to his wound herself. No record card was filled in and Tiro's teacher agreed to take him back to her house until Mma Dikobe could collect him later. The night-time journey on foot back to Bophelong had been very slow with frequent stops for Tiro to rest. Although they could have taken a taxi, Mma Dikobe thought it safer to walk. The fewer people who could identify them the better.

When Mma Dikobe finished speaking, Nono continued sitting perfectly still, her head bent forward. Slowly she raised her tired eyes:

"I thank God for that teacher and for you, Mma. But what about all those children now in the prison? Who can help their parents get them back?"

Nono paused, her bony hand stretching out to touch her grandson's arm.

"It's too hard for someone old like me to understand. You children must sleep now. Won't you sleep here with us Mma? It's late to go to your house."

Mma Dikobe thanked Nono but insisted she must return home. Before leaving she advised that Tiro stay in the house until the wound had healed enough not to be obvious.

"I shall come to check the foot tomorrow evening. But you must be careful. Someone here may be informing to the police. It would be best, Naledi, for you to say that your brother has an upset stomach."

Settling down for the second time that night, Naledi lay close to Tiro so they could whisper very quietly without Nono hearing. But they were too tired to talk for long and exhaustion soon overtook them both.

CHAPTER 17

The next morning Naledi did double her normal chores, spreading the word about Tiro's upset stomach. She explained how it had come on suddenly the previous day and he was late coming home because he felt so ill. When a child from his school asked about a police dog biting his foot, Naledi said it must have been someone else.

Walking home, balancing a full pail of water on her head, Naledi wondered whether she had lied well enough. This was quite different from any of the small childish fibs that had sometimes been part of their games. It was a horrible feeling, knowing that someone could be watching and listening at any time. Not only could you be cut down and crushed outright by an enemy coming at you like a machine, the attack could also be silent like mould creeping up the mealie cob beneath its green sheath.

As Naledi was getting ready for school, Nono spoke to her.

"Must you go today? Why don't you stay with your brother?"

Tiro was still sleeping and it was tempting to stay behind too. Perhaps there would be police waiting at the school, but that would be letting her fears get the better of her.

"I must go, but I'll be careful."

Nono turned away, appearing not to hear when Naledi said good-bye. Grabbing her hand, Dineo came trotting along beside her, as if also not wanting to let her go. Reaching the place where she used to meet Poleng, Naledi had to persuade her sister to run home.

"I'll wave," she promised and she waited until the little girl arrived back at their door, standing beneath the large white numbers.

Glancing around to see if any others were on their way to school, Naledi paused to gaze across at the charred rubble of the Sekete house. Already the fire seemed strangely distant, and yet it had happened only two weeks ago. With no other students in sight, Naledi quickened her pace, leaving the fields of village mealies and entering the veld. She sensed something was wrong as she approached the store. Students were walking away from the school.

"No school! We have to go home!" someone called to her.

Up ahead the school gates were shut and various students milled around outside. A notice stood on a rough pole inside the yard. Through the wire fencing Naledi read:

NO UNAUTHORISED PERSON
IS ALLOWED
ON THE SCHOOL PREMISES
OR
IN SCHOOL BUILDINGS
TRESPASSERS WILL BE PROSECUTED

The whole school closed! One march by the students, which they were not even allowed to complete and their school was shut down! For how long? Was this part of the removal plan? If so, the authorities would not open it again. Students outside the gates asked each other these questions in disbelief. Had Mr Molaba agreed? What about the other staff? A familiar voice intervened from the back when the discussion turned to the teachers. It was Miriam.

"I live near Mr Gwala. The police were at his house last night for more than an hour. But they didn't take him."

Perhaps the police were looking for an adult who could have helped the students organise their protest.

"They think we can't do these things by ourselves!" Naledi exclaimed. At the same time her mind flew to Rev Radebe. Had the police made that connection yet?

"They're looking for all the organisers. You should be careful," said the student from the top class to Naledi. She was the only one of the five representatives there. Theresa was probably the girl the police had snatched from the hospital. But where were Zach, Dan and Ben? No one knew.

If the police had identified the others, they must also know about her. It would be risky to go to Zach's home and he would hardly be hiding in his own house anyway. But if she went to the primary school, she might be able to speak to his brother or sister during the first break.

"They can't stop us like this! We can still do something . . ." someone began.

"They've got a lot of power, these police!"

"Okay! So let them lock us all up!"

With voices raging on all sides, Naledi slipped away. She would have to hurry if she were to reach the primary children before they went back into class. Hearing running footsteps behind her she turned to find Miriam.

"Where are you going? Can I help?"

They were in time. Play-time shouts and cries carried down the same road they had marched along yesterday. The very different shouts and cries of the day before were now a chilling memory. Arriving at the fence, Naledi called to a couple of children. Within seconds her message had been taken and Zach's sister came running over. They hadn't seen Zach since the previous morning, before the march, although a note had been put under the door during the night. It said he was okay and would come home when it was safe. Her mother had sent her to Dan's house and Dan's family had received a similar message. They had no idea where the two of them might be hiding and it was just as well because the police had raided the house in the evening. One of the police had shouted at their mother to tell him what she knew, threatening to detain the whole family. Perhaps he had realised from their expressions that they really did not know, because after turning the house upside down, they left as suddenly as they came. They were looking for 'papers' but had found nothing.

"What will you do?" Miriam asked as they left the school yard.

"They'll come for you."

Naledi was silent, her mind a battlefield. With Tiro already in danger, if she disappeared now into hiding, Nono might well have another attack. But that could also happen if she didn't hide and was arrested.

It was not a question only of Nono and the family. What were the students going to do about continuing their resistance? They could not let it be crushed just because the school had been closed. It was important to organise something outside school. They needed an organisation of young people to work with the Boomdal Resistance Committee. Bophelong also needed to prepare itself. The removal could not be stopped by talking.

Oh, there was so much to do . . .

Receiving no response to her question but seeing the anxiety in her friend's eyes, Miriam added,

"You can stay at my house. We can tell my parents that your grandmother is in hospital and you have nowhere to stay. If we tell them the police are looking for you, they might be scared to hide you."

Fear . . . It was seeping in everywhere. You had to force it out, push against it as Miriam was doing.

"Thanks, but I must go home. I can't leave Nono just like that. Maybe the police don't know everything. If they wanted me, why didn't they come last night when they were looking for Zach and Dan? Or they could have picked me up outside school this morning."

Miriam looked doubtful but Naledi had made up her mind. There were times for running away but this was not one of them.

She memorised Miriam's address, then cut across the open ground opposite Tiro's school, past the spot where she had seen him throw his well-aimed stone. Signs of yesterday's battle still lay scattered in the grass . . . a shoe, a beret, a crumpled piece of clothing perhaps torn from a shirt, stained a dark brown (was it blood?) and lying face down, a cardboard placard attached to a thin piece of wood. Naledi turned it over to see the words:

LEAVE US IN PEACE.

CHAPTER 18

Arriving at the road on the other side of the veld Naledi stopped. Why go home immediately? It was still morning. If she turned right instead of left the road led to the hospital. She could find out how many students were there and perhaps there was something she could do to help. However the thought that propelled her most strongly to the hospital was that of being with Mma Dikobe. She desperately needed to talk to her.

As she approached the hospital, Naledi realised there would probably be little chance of talking to Mma Dikobe on her own. All the nurses would be terribly busy. A long queue of people was standing and sitting alongside the wall of one of the buildings. Others, perhaps relatives, sat singly or in scattered groups on the grass in front of the long, low buildings.

Naledi was wondering where to go, when she saw a black woman in a starched white uniform hurrying along one of the paths. Running to catch up with her, she asked where Mma Dikobe could be found.

"She's in casualty over there, but you'll have to ask for her at the office. You can't just walk in there."

Naledi made her way across the grass, past an ambulance and entered the building into a small area from which corridors led off in three directions, all to rooms with closed doors. A woman sat, her scarfed head bowed, in one of the half-a-dozen chairs opposite a sign saying KANTOER – OFFICE, fixed above an opaque glass window in one of the walls. It was strangely quiet in the entrance hall. Naledi hesitated, then knocked lightly on the glass. There was a shape on the other side, but it was a little while before the glass slid open and a white face with blue eyes and shiny pink lips looked out at her.

"Yes?" the woman asked in English.

"I . . . I've come to see Mma . . . I mean Nurse Dikobe."

Naledi fumbled for the English words.

"What is it you want? She's working at the moment."

"It . . . it's personal."

The right word seemed to spring out of her mouth.

"Well, I can't promise. They're very busy in there and she's already had to leave her work once this morning to take a telephone call. Wait here and I'll see. What's your name?"

Naledi told her. At the word 'telephone', her mind had begun to buzz. Was it the lawyer with some news?

The white woman returned.

"You'll have to wait. She'll come when she's free."

Naledi thanked her and the window slid shut. She had not been told to wait outside so she sat down quietly.

Occasionally a door opened and shut and a uniformed shape appeared, then disappeared down a corridor behind another door. How foolish of her to think she could just come in and help.

At last Mma Dikobe arrived, looking concerned.

"What's wrong Naledi?"

"They shut our school, Mma. I thought I could talk to you here, and maybe help."

A fleeting smile passed across Mma Dikobe's face as she thanked Naledi, but added that it would be difficult.

"So, the school's been closed? That's a bad sign."

"Can I come to your house tonight to speak to you, Mma?"

Mma Dikobe nodded. Her strong black eyes were so reassuring, thought Naledi.

"Yes, come. I may even have a big surprise for you. This morning there was a phone call from Saul's lawyer."

Naledi held her breath.

"He's heard that Taolo and Saul have been released but he doesn't know where they are. He said the Special

Branch may bring them back here because of Saul's banning order."

"Oh Mma! That's wonderful news!"

Naledi flung her arms round Mma Dikobe and hugged her. It was a hug that very nearly became a heaving sob. The woman waiting on the chair had lifted her sad, tired eyes for a moment to look at the two of them and a pang of guilt shot through Naledi. Could you realiy be happy about anything in the middle of all this terror?

With a deep breath Naledi gained control of herself, at the same time feeling Mma Dikobe's hand on her shoulder gently leading her a little way down the corridor.

"There's something you can do before you go, Naledi," she said keeping her voice low.

"That lady there is the mother of the girl with the bad head injury – the one the police snatched from us yesterday for questioning. They brought her back in the middle of the night completely unconscious. The doctor says her skull is fractured. Those devils may have hit her some more. Her mother's been waiting here from early this morning. Can you sit with her for a while?"

As Mma Dikobe disappeared through one of the doors, Naledi returned to the small waiting area.

"Intshwarele, Mma, excuse me, are you not Theresa's mother?"

The woman looked up, her eyes answering yes. Naledi sat down beside her.

"I'm a friend of Theresa, Mma."

It was difficult to know what to say, but slowly Naledi found the words and gradually Theresa's mother warmed to her, and spoke of some of her fears. She knew of people being paralysed for life from fractured skulls, unable to move or even talk. Yesterday morning she had said good-bye to a healthy, smiling daughter and this morning that same girl was lying almost lifeless, with a broken head.

"What kind of people can do this?" she cried.

There was little comfort Naledi could offer to stem her hot tears.

CHAPTER 19

Telling Nono about the school closure was not easy. Her grandmother stood beside the table, her bony, wrinkled fingers grasping the wooden top like gnarled roots of an old tree when the ground is giving way beneath it. Naledi had to help her to a chair.

Nono, who had never been to school herself had managed to keep their father in school for only three years when he was young. There had been no money for more, even though Nono saw education as the only way out of poverty. Naledi remembered clearly the story her grandmother had told her before she had set off for her first day at school. It was about a dry barren land where the only place plants grew well was alongside a narrow river. It was difficult for other plants to get near to the river because the space was so limited and precious. Nono had said that school was like the river, offering its water only to those lucky few who could stay beside it. Naledi's mother wanted to do all she could to keep her children beside the river, and in turn they would have to work very hard to drink as much from it as possible.

How could Nono understand the students' feelings? Although she was so worried by the idea of removal, she still could not accept that young people should risk precious schooling by trying to resist. Nor could Nono accept that students should dare to criticize how they were being taught. When Naledi had once repeated her grandmother's story to Taolo, he had exclaimed,

"Yes, but the river is poisoned! Why must we learn Afrikaans and just those things the gov'ment want us to know? A gov'ment we can't even vote for! So they can keep us where they want for ever! No! We must get to the source of the river, clean it up and dig new courses for it. Then we'll send it all over the dry land!"

Whenever he referred to the government, he sneered at the very word.

If Nono had reacted with something like, "See what this foolishness has brought?" Naledi would have once more tried to explain. Instead Nono responded with silence which Naledi found even worse to cope with. But ignoring Nono's silence, Tiro asked Naledi outright,

"Did you go to my school? Is it also closed?"

When Naledi shook her head, he pulled a face, sucking the air through his teeth, before going back to his game in the adjoining room with Dineo.

Naledi sat down to eat a little cold pap. Her last proper meal had been the night before and she was hungry. She hurried, not enjoying her food. Only Dineo seemed able to ignore the tension, laughing at the shapes Tiro was making for her with a piece of wire. Swallowing her last mouthful, Naledi said she was going to collect more firewood. Their stock was running low and although it was too late to make the long trip all the way to the best place for finding dead branches, she would walk along the dry river-bed where she might find a few small sticks and twigs from bushes and small trees at the side.

When no-one else was there, the river-bed was one place where Naledi always felt at peace. She dimly remembered the time when it had been flowing with water. That was before the white farmer had dammed the water further upstream, using it to irrigate his farm. Villagers still spoke of their shock at losing their water supply. Until the pipe-line had been laid to the village, they had to make the long journey with buckets to the white farm to buy water that they had once freely taken from the river. Even now water from the village tap still had to be paid for through a levy on every household. The Chief then took a lump sum to the farmer. What would happen now Chief Sekete had gone, Naledi wondered? For how long could they continue with this disarray?

The afternoon sun was beginning to lose its heat as Naledi wandered over the fine pale sand of the dry bed, picking her way over the smooth grey-brown pebbles. Allowing herself to forget her worries, she became absorbed in the task of scouring the long grass at the side and gathering up twigs which had fallen into the bed from overhanging branches. It was another world down here, enveloped in the quiet of the veld except for the sounds of birds and the cicadas, and the occasional lowing of cattle or bark of a dog. There was one stretch of the winding bed that had special memories, where Naledi always looked to see if the rocks were still arranged in a particular order. Here she and her friends had played 'house' when they were little. They had built their own small settlement and up until now the rings of rocks had remained intact, untouched by the upheavals of their lives.

On the way back, her bundle of sticks on her head, Naledi took a spur of the moment decision to make a detour towards the Dikobe house. Using one hand to steady the bundle, she quickened her pace. Would Taolo and his father have returned? Approaching the house her hopes fell when she saw that neither the door nor the windows were open. There would surely have been some sign of life if they were inside. The peace of the river-bed lost, Naledi turned towards home.

First stacking her bundle of sticks outside the door, Naledi went into the dimly-lit room. Mma Dikobe had already arrived, as promised, to check Tiro's foot. She did not have time to chat with Nono this time. It was obvious she was in a hurry to be on her way home. She set about examining the wound in a business-like way, rather as if she were still in the hospital. Nono must have noticed because she started to say something and then stopped. The task completed, Mma Dikobe sensed that Nono was feeling a little hurt. She apologised.

"Forgive me, Mma. I have something on my mind right now and I must hurry. If Naledi comes with me, she can collect some more bandage from my house. Then she can change it for her brother tomorrow. The foot is healing nicely."

Mma Dikobe was amazing! Even with her mind so occupied, she had remembered that Naledi wanted to talk to her! But as they walked through the rapidly darkening village, Naledi suddenly felt it would be unfair to burden Mma Dikobe with her worries. This was not the right moment. Mma Dikobe's mind must be absorbed by the possibility of her son and husband returning at any moment. And what state would they be in?

Once the sun went down it did not take long for night to descend in all its thickness. Naledi carried the torch her mother had given them as a special present, but she did not switch it on. They would reach the Dikobe house before the deepening purple gave way to black. Flickers of orange and red lit up the doorways and windows of the shadow-filled houses, and clouds of smoke billowed into the surrounding yards, before rising and merging into the haze of the coming night. Exchanging quick greetings with passers-by, they identified voices rather than faces. Naledi slipped her arm through Mma Dikobe's as they hurried their steps, peering ahead to the house. No . . . no lights, no open door . . .

Inside, Mma Dikobe lit the lamp. The room looked so

lonely and empty. So this is what it is like to spend your nights completely alone, thought Naledi. The house was large compared with Nono's, with three rooms leading off the main one. On a sideboard lay some knitting, a few books and a radio. Mma Dikobe obviously kept herself busy. She was already moving around the room briskly, preparing to light the coal stove.

"I can do it for you, Mma," offered Naledi.

Little flames were just coming to life when Naledi thought she hard the sound of a motor. They both went to the door. Yes, there were the headlights of a car in the distance! Quickly Mma Dikobe pulled Naledi back.

"It's better the police don't see you here!"

"I'll go round the back!"

Slipping past Mma Dikobe, Naledi hurried outside to the rear of the house and crouched next to a bin against the wall. The car was definitely coming closer. Before long there was the sound of the vehicle stopping with doors opening. A loud rough voice announced in English,

"You didn't think you'd see this place so soon, did you, hey? We're being good to you. But any nonsense and you'll be back on those cold cement floors before you can say your own name!"

There was no reply. Naledi heard only the silence of the night and her own heart beating very fast.

"Well, hello Mrs Dikobe!" The voice turned to a sneer.

"Aren't you going to greet your husband and son?"

"I can wait until you leave."

Whatever she was feeling, Mma Dikobe's voice was calm.

"It seems we're not welcome here, gentlemen! I thought the lady would thank us for returning her family!"

"Hell, I wouldn't want to stay in this dump if you paid me . . . and these people are making such a fuss about leaving it!"

"Agh man, they don't know what's good for them."

"One last word. Your husband is under twenty-four hour house arrest so he must entertain himself inside this fence. And remember, our eyes and ears are everywhere. Every move you make, even in a little place like this, we'll know about it!"

"Kom! Let's go!"

There was a slamming of doors, the revving of an engine, the sound of a car manoeuvring and finally a screeching of tyres as it set off back up the track. Naledi stayed where she was for a little longer until the car-lights were in line with the light from Rra Thopi's house and the general hush confirmed that the police were truly gone. She came out from her hiding place to find the Dikobe family in a close embrace. Taolo was the first to see her.

"Hey sis! How's it? So you were hiding here!"

Both Taolo and his father hugged Naledi in turn. Rra Dikobe looked terribly tired, but his grip was strong and steady.

"I'll be going home now, Mma. Shall I take the bandage?"

The policeman's words about 'eyes and ears', as well as Rra Dikobe's banning order, should not be lightly ignored.

As Naledi set off with her torch and the bandage, Taolo ran up beside her.

"Shouldn't you stay to talk with your mother?"

"Let them be alone together for a while! I won't be long. I'm only walking to your home. You know I missed you."

Taolo's directness startled her.

"How was it in there?"

He was quiet for a moment, then stopped walking. They were in the dark stretch of veld separating them from the nearest house. Naledi halted, her torch flickering ahead over the cracks and grooves in the track.

"Compared to some of the others, I had it easy," he said, folding his arms, "and you'll find me tougher than ever. Those swines think they can break you. But it's the opposite! Every minute in there, you think about them, and you question, 'What should we have done? What should we do now? What can we do next time?' And when others are with you, you begin to make plans. Even when they try to break you, you go on planning."

Naledi remained quiet while he paused:

"They made me stand for three days and nights on one spot . . . but no. I don't feel sorry for myself! Even if they detain me for ever, that's no problem, I'm ready for it. They can kill me, and lots of others, but we'll get what we want in the end, to live like free people. One thing I learnt in there is that being locked in jail isn't much different from the way we are locked up outside. We are all handcuffed!"

Taking the bandage parcel from Naledi, he held on to her hand as they set off again following the bobbing circle of light along the path. She had not expected this, but quickly warming to the hand's firm grasp, she began to tell Taolo about what had happened at the school.

Close to the church, Mma Tshadi's voice slicing through the dark, took them by surprise and they let go of each other's hands. Mma Tshadi's large figure appeared behind a torch, breathing rather heavily from the effort of hurrying. She had heard and seen the car, and guessed it was something to do with the Dikobes. Delighted to hear that both father and son had returned, she told Taolo that she had not been idle. She had written to the white magistrate asking to see him with a couple of village elders so they could discuss the removal. As yet there had been no reply. However from her conversations with people in the village, it seemed that everyone wanted Saul Dikobe to represent them in the matter of the removal. They were not put off by the banning order and would use Taolo and his mother for carrying messages between them. If Rra Dikobe was agreeable, by tomorrow she would have a petition ready which villagers would sign, asking the magistrate to allow them to appoint him as their representative since their chief had deserted them. In the meantime if Rra Dikobe could outline his plans for resistance to Taolo and his mother, they would hold a meeting to discuss them.

By the time they reached Nono's house, Naledi and Taolo had offered to help Mma Tshadi take the petition around. Taolo refused to be intimidated by the 'eyes and ears' threat, telling Naledi that he believed the police were really after someone else. From his interrogation, he had gathered that they thought an underground group was responsible for burning down Sekete's house. If freedom-fighters were in the area, it was possible that the police had released them simply as decoys, hoping that the guerillas would make contact with them. In the meantime, it was important not to lose any time planning resistance to the removal.

Arriving at the entrance to the yard, Naledi remembered David Sadire. What had happened to him and why hadn't he been released too? The tale was sombre. According to rumours in jail, David had been taken away to a psychiatric hospital. Taolo had last seen him after David had been returned to the cell following a second interrogation, this time badly tortured. Burn marks on his body indicated the police had used electric wires. The boy could not say anything, and it seemed that he had lost his mind. The next day he had been removed from the cell and never returned.

"He was always so quiet! What information could he have?" Naledi protested in a whisper.

"After the first interrogation, he said the police kept asking him about Jerry Kau. They were good friends before Jerry left school for the mines."

So the police did suspect that Mma Kau's son was connected with the fire and the freedom-fighters. No wonder Mma Kau was worried. The police had destroyed the quiet David just because he was Jerry's friend. What would they do to Jerry if they caught him? That day outside the chief's house his eyes had carried the same fiery defiant message as Taolo's words.

Insisting that Taolo take the torch back with him, Naledi said softly before crossing the yard,

"Come in the morning! We can go to Mma Tshadi's together."

CHAPTER 20

The return of Saul Dikobe and his son brought a new mood to Bophelong. People who previously wanted nothing to do with them now saw them as offering their only hope to fight the removal. Even after being carted off to jail, Saul Dikobe was still prepared to resist and help. Within two days, Mma Tshadi's petition was completed and delivered by hand to the magistrate's office in the white town. It was accompanied by another letter from Mma Tshadi again requesting an interview with the magistrate, so that she and other village elders could hear his reply.

It surprised Naledi to see how most people in the village were managing to get on with their everyday lives. The absence of a chief to attend to official matters and disputes had not yet begun to have a noticeable effect, and although the closure of the secondary school was a serious shock, initially village life continued as if students were at home on holiday. With the recent rains encouraging weeds as well as crops, there was plenty to do in the fields.

Nor did the thought that the government was trying to force them to leave their fields, stop the villagers from tending to them. Naledi noticed their reaction was quite the reverse. There was a fierce and angry pride at being able to work this soil with little more than the strength of their own hands. Now white people, wanting the land back again, had ordered that the people who had struggled and survived there for all those years were to be dug out with bulldozers and thrown aside, as if they were nothing but weeds.

Up at the white farm where she had come to take Nono's place, Naledi pulled at real weeds with her hoe, watching the soil crumble with each stroke. Across the lawn, cropped so smoothly that it appeared to be a green blanket, stood the long fine house, settled and secure, surrounded by its own grove of trees. Her heart burnt with intense anger at the injustice of it all. A letter had also come from Mma in Jo'burg. The white 'Madam' for whom she worked was not prepared to let her return home at the moment. She would have to wait and ask the 'Madam' again in a week or two.

It was, however, on the day when their pensions were refused, the villagers truly realised that the pattern of their lives was being changed for ever. Since most of the adults in the village were pensioners, without that money, even that small sum, how could they survive?

A week after Mma Tshadi had delivered the petition, Mma Kau and Nono were among those who set out at first light on pension day to make the tiring journey to Boomdal. Nono insisted she was well enough to go as long as they walked slowly. Tiro's foot was much better but he stayed at home, minding Dineo. As usual Naledi accompanied her grandmother, but today instead of being able to go on to school, she stood with Nono in the long queue, waiting patiently for the office to be opened. The sun's heat reflected off the white walls of the building and soon penetrated the pavement underfoot. There was no shade either. Many pensioners lived much nearer in Boomdal itself and were at the head of the queue. It was not uncommon for Nono and others from outlying areas to have to wait a few hours before their turn would come for papers to be checked and the money dished out roughly, like scraps to a dog.

About three hours later, the first of the Bophelong pensioners reached the desk, only to be turned away and told his money was no longer at that office. It was waiting for him in Bop. The old man stood by the desk looking dazed, not understanding while an official called for the next person. When the old man did not move, a policeman in khaki pulled him aside, telling him loudly to go home. The news spread rapidly down the line. The group of people refused their pensions grew all the time, gathering a short distance away from the policeman. Yet each of the remaining villagers continued to wait for his or her turn to reach the desk, to watch the hands reject the paper and the lips to mouth the words:

"This can only be paid to you in Bophuthatswana. Next!"

Thoughts spinning furiously, Naledi edged forwards besides her grandmother. Like the others, Nono seemed set on hearing the words spoken directly to her. At last they were standing before the white official. Naledi stared intently at him, trying to catch his attention, but his eyes looked right through them. However, before he could shout 'Next!', she interrupted.

"How can my grandmother go there? She's ill! Look at her and see for yourself! Where will she get money for food?'

Naledi felt herself grasped on both sides. Nono's fingers were pressing hard into her right arm, telling her to calm down, while a large violent hand pulled at her left shoulder.

"Out of the way! Take your grandmother and leave!"

She wanted to shake her shoulders to get free, but Nono was holding on to her arm and would have tumbled. Instead she glared into the face under the policeman's cap. It was covered with tiny beads of sweat glistening on his brown skin. The round black pupils showed no expression.

"Is this how you treat your own grandmother? Chasing her like a stray donkey?"

Naledi could hear her voice rising sharply. She wanted to scream at the policeman, at the official behind the desk, at the whole lot of them who were working to destroy their lives.

"Are we animals? Why must . . ."

"Please, Naledi, please my child . . . come quietly!" Nono's tone was urgent, pleading. "Don't make more trouble for us! Let's go and talk this thing out at home. Come child!"

With each word Nono's breathing was becoming heavier. Naledi forced herself to swallow, stopping up the tirade she wanted to unleash. Seeing what was happening, people in the queue quickly made space for Nono to sit down so she could lean against the wall. Naledi lowered her grandmother to the pavement, helped by Mma Kau who had given up her place in the queue. Nono refused the suggestion that they take her to the hospital, adamant that all she needed was a little rest. Usually, after collecting her money, she would walk to the general store to buy mealie meal, sugar, beans and other provisions. Then she would sit outside the store along with others who had school-going grandchildren, waiting for them to arrive from school to help carry the parcels home.

But today there was no money and no question of going to the shop. By this time of the month you could see the bottom of each of the food containers at home. Mma sent money every second month, in between the pension payments. How would they manage until then? Most families would be in the same position. The powerful, terrible machine that was bent on destroying their homes now intended to starve them out.

The journey back to Bophelong was made with empty hands, on empty stomachs. Instead of the satisfaction of feeling they had survived yet another month and that the parcels being carried were the means of surviving the next, there was a sense of numbness and bitter resentment. Mma Kau and Naledi, one on each side of Nono, trailed behind the returning villagers. When one of the women walking slowly with them started to sing quietly, the others gradually joined in. She began with a song about a father who had to leave his family behind, in order to search for work in the city. It was a story they all knew too well and the tune expressed for them the anguish of their own hearts.

At first Naledi found the singing calmed her, somehow making the pain bearable, but as it continued, she realised that she wanted to scream as she had done at the pension office – before stopping for Nono's sake. Or if not to scream, she wanted to sing angry songs. Songs that could at least hit out at those who were crushing them. Swallowing hard and pressing in her lips tightly, she completed the journey beside Nono in silence.

Finally reaching the village, they found Mma Tshadi in the centre of a group of pensioners outside the church. Taolo was sitting to one side on the church yard wall, listening. Naledi saw his eyes smile briefly towards her as she led Nono to rest against the wall. The discussion was heated, someone putting forward the idea of going into Bop just to collect their money. It would mean wasting quite a bit of it on the bus-fare, but wouldn't that be better than having nothing?

Perhaps it would be cheaper to hire something like a van or a truck, suggested Mma Tshadi. They could pay a deposit in advance, then the remainder once they had collected their money. Hesitant because they had never done anything like this before, the pensioners still thought it was a good idea – and they could see no other way out of the trap. Looking over to Taolo and Naledi with a determined smile, Mma Tshadi said,

"I'm sure these two young people will help. If they go to the town tomorrow, they can ask how much it costs."

"Can I, Nono?" Naledi asked immediately.

Nono's face was covered by her hand, revealing only small sags of wrinkled skin. Without looking up, she nodded.

"I'll come early," promised Taolo.

Exhausted, Nono went to bed as soon as they were home and Naledi prepared the meal, cooking half the usual amount of mealie meal. She would save the beans for tomorrow, then they might just get two more meals. After that there would be nothing. It would be necessary to write another letter to Mma, in case something went wrong with the plan for the trip into Bop to collect the pensions. But even if Mama were able to send a little money in advance, the post was slow and there would be a delay.

After their brief meal, Naledi cleared the table to write. She did not want to be long over it, as it meant keeping on the lamp and once the paraffin was used up, there was no more to replace it. The others had gone straight to bed. Dineo whining and crying that she was still hungry. Tiro's appetite was obviously unsatisfied, but he said nothing. In the letter Naledi kept to the bare facts about the pension money and also mentioned that their school had been closed. But she wrote nothing about the demonstration or about the police dog biting Tiro. It was only when she came to sign 'Your loving daughter' that she could not stop the old ache from missing her mother surging up within her, pushing sharply against her rib-cage.

Turning off the lamp and feeling her way to her sleeping mat, Naledi thought about the next day. She was looking forward to being with Taolo. He had not held her hand again since that night of his return, but on the occasions they had been together, she had felt somehow revived. It was as if their minds were breathing together.

CHAPTER 21

The following morning Taolo came running with news that changed their plans. Three people had arrived from the Anti-Removal Committee and were waiting in the church hall to interview the villagers. While in Johannesburg, his mother had apparently gone to the offices of this organisation to tell them about Bophelong. Promising to come as soon as possible, they had asked that nothing be said about the visit in advance, in case the police tried to stop it. His mother had kept it a secret even from him. Now members of the Committee had arrived, it was important for them to talk to as many people as possible. They needed to gather information about how long each family had been living at Bophelong, what sort of agreements had been made about the land, whether there were any papers and so on. Suggesting that Naledi and Mma Tshadi go round the village telling people to go to the church, Taolo said he would go ahead on his own with arranging the transport to collect the pensions.

"My foot is better. I want to go too," Tiro said to his grandmother.

Nono made no objection. Could she be changing

wondered Naledi?

Entering the church hall, out of breath, both brother and sister were startled for the first few moments. Inside, sitting at the table from which Chief Sekete had given his speech, were two men and a woman, but the woman and one of the men were white. Almost the only white people who came to the village were police or government officials.

Naledi and Tiro hesitated at the door, until Mma Dikobe, standing by the table, saw them and beckoned.

"These people are from the Anti-Removal Committee and they don't have much time. Can you start by calling Mma Tshadi to meet them and then work your way around the village? Try not to be obvious, and it's best you don't call Rra Thopi."

"Why is that, Mma?" asked Naledi.

"Someone is informing the police and he's the only one who can see our house from where he lives. We're not certain, but it could be him. So we'll try to keep him out of this. Of course, if he turns up, we'll just have to let him in."

Naledi looked again at the strangers. Smiling across at her, both the white people seemed young and a little nervous. The woman had a short fringe and straight brown hair which bobbed lightly whenever she turned her head. Their black companion was thoroughly at ease. He sported a neat beard and moustache and a smile which seemed to be hiding at the corners of his mouth as he winked at the children.

"They don't bite you know! Come on Annie, you'd better talk to them or they might go round telling people some white monsters have come to Bophelong!"

The woman called Annie grinned rather shyly.

"Dumela! O tsogile jang?" She greeted them in perfect Tswana.

Her black companion's face broke into a broad smile at Naledi's and Tiro's expressions.

"She knows a lot more than that too, you know!" he said in a deep voice in Tswana, laughing. He switched back to English.

"But this one here, my friend Mike, is still no good! That's why I have come to translate for him."

He slapped the back of the young white man whose round pink cheeks deepened, clashing in colour with his bush of ginger hair.

"Hullo!" Mike said in English. "Joe's right. He's been trying to teach me Tswana, but I keep forgetting."

"Rubbish! You just make excuses!" boomed Joe. "But we mustn't keep you children. Please bring Mrs. Tshadi quickly. We must start our work!"

The rest of the day was spent in carrying messages and explaining to people why they were needed in the church hall. Since no-one had ever heard of this Committee before, Naledi and Tiro found themselves faced with all sorts of questions to which they had no answers: How can they help us? Are they friends with the government? Can they make the government change its mind? The villagers still came though, and were further surprised when they saw that two of the interviewers were white. They were persuaded to come forward only by seeing Mma Dikobe sitting with them and by Mma Tshadi's recommendation. She told everyone how the white woman had listened carefully to her and written down everything she had said.

It would have been impossible to keep secret what was happening inside the church. Apart from the strange car parked at the back, anyone passing could hear the sound of many voices. After their interviews, people stayed around discussing the questions they had been asked. They were also waiting for the Committee to address them and tell them their plans.

At first, Naledi and Tiro called on the villagers who lived furthest away from Rra Thopi, until Tiro decided to go by his house and see what he was doing. Racing back to Naledi, he brought the news that they did not need to worry about Rra Thopi at all. According to his youngest daughter, her father had set off early that morning with his cattle. He was taking them to his brother who had land about a day's journey away. When Tiro asked the little girl why her father was doing this, she replied,

"So they won't be killed when we move to the new place."

That was ominous. None of the other villagers who owned cattle had done anything with them yet. People had been saying, quite simply,

"How can we move when we have our cattle here?"

At the meeting Chief Sekete had avoided answering the questions about land for grazing cattle and cultivating crops. Here at Bophelong, although only tenants on Sekete land, they always had use of the surrounding veld in return for a small payment. If Rra Thopi was moving his cattle, perhaps he knew more than the rest of them. Mma Dikobe and the Committee would be interested in that.

In the middle of the afternoon, Tiro brought Nono up to the church. She told the white woman when the family had first come to Bophelong and what their present circumstances were. The story Nono told was one the children knew well – how their father's father saved the life of Chief Sekete's father when he was wounded in North Africa. They were together there as stretcher bearers with the South African troops who were fighting in the desert against the Germans in the World War. When Chief Sekete's father was wounded, their own grandfather risked heavy gunfire and shelling to get him back behind their own lines. After the war, Chief Sekete's father offered their grandfather a plot on which to build a house, as well as a couple of beasts. It was land which the Sekete family had bought many years earlier before the law which stopped black people buying land in most places. While Chief Sekete's father and their grandfather were alive, their family never had to pay rent. But after both the old men died, the present chief began to ask their father to pay, saying that he needed money for his growing family. Their father had not wanted to argue. Nor were there any papers to show that their grandfather had been given the land.

Nono felt in her pocket. She had a little card, which she had kept very carefully. It had been given to her husband on his discharge from the army. Shakily Nono handed the tattered paper to the white woman. It was from the white Prime Minister of the day and had a 'V' at the top:

> V
> WELCOME
> HOME!
>
> I wish to bid you a very hearty welcome home, after your long absence and arduous labours. I hope you enjoy your stay in the future country and be refreshed for the work which lies ahead wherever it may be.
>
> J. Smuts

The white woman's brown hair bobbed as she quietly shook her head over the letter. Nono continued the story, relating first how her husband, who had developed back problems during the war, was unable to get any compensation when he could no longer work because of the pain. She had supported the family herself with her meagre earnings from labouring on local white farms and the few crops they grew for themselves at Bophelong. Money problems had forced them to sell their animals after her husband's death.

When her son was sixteen he enlisted in the mines and sent home a little money each month. After he married, his wife earned money working for a white family in the city, so Nono had brought up her son's children. Then her son had died from the 'coughing sickness' which he caught in the mines. Since then she and the children had been entirely dependent on her small pension – which she had been refused yesterday – and the money the children's mother sent from Jo'burg. When she finished her story the three at the table remained silent in sympathy. Nono seemed to have spent all her breath. Tiro helped her home.

By the end of the day, there were still a few people who had not been interviewed. Nor had there been any time for a general discussion. Joe and his two white companions said they would continue the following day, but it would be risky for them to seek accommodation elsewhere.

"Even if we split up and my white friends here go to a select hotel in their whites-only reserve, it's dangerous. In these country towns everyone pokes their nose into a stranger's business. Anyway, these two aren't good enough liars!"

It was the second time Naledi heard him boom into laughter. His reference to 'a select hotel in their whites-only reserve' carried a clear mocking tone. It was strange, thought Naledi, because he and his two white companions really seemed to like each other and they laughed together at his jokes about them and the 'white reserve'. But while Joe appeared totally unflustered by the dangers he was talking about, Mike and Annie were not able to conceal the signs of worry in their eyes. Yet white people usually seemed so sure of themselves – the 'Madam' for whom their mother worked, the 'Missus' for whom Nono worked, the shop assistants in the white town who always served their white customers first and did not want you to touch anything until you had bought it. In fact the white people Naledi had come across usually seemed so arrogant.

Mma Tshadi solved the problem, offering to accommodate the three Committee workers in her house for the night. Annie thanked Mma Tshadi warmly, admitting that they would be in trouble without the generosity of the people they visited. They carried sleeping bags with them in their car.

The sun was sinking behind the horizon as Naledi and Tiro hurried home. Taolo had not yet returned and Naledi was beginning to worry about him. After he fixed the arrangements for the transport, he might have gone looking for some of his friends. Would he find out where Zach and the others were? Or had the police already found them? With these questions unanswered, and others thrown up by the day's events, Naledi knew she was in for another restless night.

CHAPTER 22

Taolo was talking to Joe at the back of the church-hall when Naledi and Tiro arrived in the morning. A couple of children at the water-tap had already told Naledi they had seen him earlier on. Hearing that was like having a tight strap removed from around her chest. But the ache gripping her stomach remained. Their evening meal had again been halved.

She wanted to hurry over to Taolo, but restrained herself. He glanced towards the door as she entered, giving a slight nod, then continued talking. Nearby, sitting in a circle and leaning forward deep in conversation so their heads were almost touching were Mma Dikobe,

Mma Tshadi, the two white people and a man with his back to the door.

From the top end of the hall Mma Kau greeted the children as she spread a white cloth over the table. She beckoned to Tiro to come and help. Two other women were straightening the benches. Of course, it was Sunday. With the usual routine of their lives upset, Naledi had lost track of the days. Had Nono also forgotten it was Sunday? Normally she would never miss a Sunday service. But this morning she had remained in bed, still exhausted from the trip to Boomdal for the pension and then the Committee interview. Recalling and relating the whole family history appeared to have completely drained her.

Moving into the hall, Naledi looked once more at the man with his back to the door and recognised the bush of hair. It was Rev Radebe! At the same time, Mma Dikobe looked up. Glancing at her watch, she exclaimed,

"My goodness! It will be time for the service soon. Come here, Naledi!" Taking Naledi's hand, she continued. "Reverend, this child was one of those elected to represent the students at the secondary school. I'm sure she would be pleased to hear about some of her friends."

Rev Radebe sprang up from his seat. Grasping Naledi's free hand in both of his, he shook it keenly. The energy of his eyes and hands was infectious.

"I expect you know from Mma Dikobe that your friend Theresa is still critical. But for the moment your other friends on the committee are all right. They're trying to keep their heads low until things are quieter, but I hear they've been very busy!"

He smiled broadly, little furrows crinkling around his eyes and mouth.

"The latest I hear is that there is now a Boomdal Youth Association – the B.Y.A. – and your friends intend organising the young people to join in with our Resistance Committee."

"Can you get a message to them Rra? We need to meet them."

Naledi shot a glance towards Taolo. Rev Radebe nodded.

"I don't think you need me. You'll find your friend has managed to see them yesterday. But now, you must excuse me. I must get ready for the service." He hurried through the benches towards Mma Kau.

Seeing other villagers beginning to arrive, Naledi wondered whether she should run home to see if Nono wished to come. But perhaps it was better to leave her resting. It wasn't simply her body that was failing – her spirits seemed to be failing too.

"Deep in thought, hey sis! Take a seat." Taolo's voice brought her back from her thoughts of Nono. They sat at the far end of a bench where they could talk quietly. He had managed to see Zach, Dan and Ben. Although they were still in hiding, they were planning a meeting where their campaign would be decided. When the place and date were decided, someone would come to Bophelong to let them know. Because there had been no suitable vehicles for hire in Boomdal, Taolo had had to go all the way into the white town to arrange transport into Bop on Monday for the pensions. It was expensive so he had then had to go back into Boomdal to ask Rev Radebe's help in advancing the money. Every pensioner would have to contribute ten rand – a large slice out of a small pension – to pay for hiring a truck. When the owner had enquired about the reason for the trip, Taolo had just told him that the villagers wanted to see the place they were being moved to. The man had not probed any deeper and from their conversation, Taolo had been surprised to discover that not all the town's white people were in favour of the removal. Many of the shop-keepers would lose customers since Boomdal people often shopped in the white town where many of them worked. He laughed.

"When it comes to money, it's funny there's no colour problem for them!"

Rev Radebe's voice interrupted them. "Welcome, my brothers and sisters, in this time of trial. Today we have some special visitors."

The service was about to begin. It turned out to be fervent and inspiring. Yet again Reverend Radebe used words and hymns to carry extra meaning. Hope. Determination. He asked them to look at the solid rocks in the stone walls around them, reminding them of the vision and labours of their ancestors in constructing such a sturdy building for the place in which they would renew their spirits each week. They must have brought those great stones on waggons from a distant region, confident that their efforts were not just for themselves but their descendants. They had a stake in this land. As they sang and Naledi let her voice and heart fly up – as if free for a few moments – into the rafters of the old church, she regretted not having collected Nono. Surely even Nono's heart would have been revived.

Immediately after the service the three visitors addressed the congregation. Joe did most of the speaking.

"My friends, we can't tell you what you should do. But we can tell you how others have tried to resist and what methods they used. Every place is different, but one thing is certain. The only way to stay where you are is to stay completely united!" He emphasized each of the last three words, then paused.

"The first thing the authorities always do, is to make divisions among you. They will offer one person something, another one something else, put pressure on the next – and before you know it, people will be going. That makes it impossible for those who want to stay."

The rising murmur from the audience told Joe they understood.

Explaining which laws would be used to move the people of Bophelong and Boomdal, Joe predicted that the government would act against the villagers first because they were regarded in law as 'squatters'. Only the Sekete family would get any compensation for the land. Nor were there any laws to which the villagers could appeal. Probably their only hope was to get publicity, to get their story into the newspapers because the government did not like people from other countries hearing about these evictions. Indeed the Minister of 'Co-operation and Development' – Joe said it with a sneer – had stated to the world that no-one in South Africa was forced to move to a 'homeland'. Everyone chose to go!

Some people laughed in disbelief, others shouted angrily and others simply shook their heads silently. Another heated discussion followed. It was decided that Mma Tshadi should not wait any longer for a reply from the magistrate but go to his office herself the next day and demand an interview. Taolo was to accompany her. If the magistrate refused to let Rra Dikobe represent them (which seemed likely), then at least he should let them appoint someone else they trusted. In the meantime Mma Tshadi and the Dikobes would draw up two letters – one to be sent to the Minister and the other to a national newspaper so many people would hear about their problem.

The rest of the day passed quickly, with the Committee workers completing their interviews. As the afternoon wore on, however, Naledi felt increasingly tired. As they watched Joe and his friends disappear across the veld in their car, the painful grip around her stomach became so tight, she felt it could not be pulled in any further. Something must have showed in her face because Mma Dikobe came and spoke to her. Naledi was reluctant to speak of their difficulty, feeling sure that they were not alone in going hungry. But when Mma Dikobe uncovered the truth, she insisted that Naledi come and take some mealie meal and beans from her.

On Naledi's way with Taolo and his mother to the Dikobe's house they noticed Rra Thopi had returned from his cattle journey. He was leaning against his wall watching them. Had he arrived back in time to see the car leaving the church or had his children said anything to him?

That evening they made plans for the following morning. Tiro would accompany Nono in the truck to Bop, while Naledi would go to the farm again to do Nono's work. Dineo would have to come with her as Mma Kau would also be away collecting her pension. seeing Nono looking a little brighter, Naledi told her about the meeting and that Mma Tshadi was hoping to see the magistrate. Tomorrow was going to be a busy day for everyone. The village would be left almost empty, apart from Saul and a few boys minding the animals.

CHAPTER 23

No one was prepared for the sight that met them on their return to the village late the following afternoon. Above the high-pitched buzz of invisible cicadas in the grass, Naledi heard an engine as she tramped wearily past the mealie fields and Rra Thopi's empty cattle enclosure on her way back from the white farm. Perhaps it was the hired truck. A different sound now followed, something between wailing and shouting. Naledi tried to speed up but it had been a long, hard day and the child on her back slowed her down.

As the path rose up a slight incline, the centre of the village came into view. Where was the church? Instead there were only two roofless, broken walls with great jagged holes for windows. Where Taolo had been standing at the back of the hall the day before, there was nothing, just a great pile of rubble. A short distance away stood an enormous yellow bulldozer like a great monster with its ugly metal jaw hanging open. The pensioners who had just climbed out of their large truck stared in dismay. The parcels in their hands showed that they had at least got their money.

Naledi forgot her weariness and ran, Dineo jogging up and down on her back. Strewn among the stones were wooden beams, window frames, benches, a door with protruding hinges. Clumps of thatch lay everywhere. Even the mud wall surrounding the yard was in ruins.

Naledi found Nono sitting on a pile of stones, staring blankly at the wreckage through watery eyes. She was not crying but seemed lost in a lament-like humming. Only some boys who had been herding cattle not far from the village had seen what had happened. They told how two army trucks – one carrying the bulldozer, had arrived in the morning. They had watched as the men in the giant machine had rammed and wrecked their church. A couple of white men in uniform had given the orders to a group of black men who had first of all scrambled up onto the roof and begun hacking it away. The boys had called out.

"Why are you breaking our church?"

But the reply had come in a language they did not understand.

One or two of the wreckers had even seemed to be joking with each other as they slung great handfuls of thatch down to the yard, chaff and dust flying everywhere. But most had just got on with the job quite grimly. There had been no adults the children could warn, no one except Rra Dikobe who was not supposed to leave his own yard. In fact they saw him on top of the small rise, observing the destruction. The children had stayed to watch, so close to the church-yard wall that they had had to protect their eyes from chips of splintering stones. The machine had completed what the men had begun, smashing and crushing the once solid rocks. At last the bulldozer had been parked to one side and the army trucks had roared away. They said that Rra Dikobe had watched until the end.

The villagers listened intently to the boys' tale, and as evening approached nobody seemed ready to leave. Then Rra Rampou stooped down and slowly picked up a stone from the pile behind Nono. He put it in place on the smashed wall, and went back to the pile. Naledi could see the effort in his face as he collected the next stone. A woman called out,

"We shall build again!"

Putting down her parcels, she joined the old man. Immediately others began to follow suit. Naledi gently led Nono aside so she would not be in the way. Children were asked to pile up the scattered thatch on one side of the yard. Tiro worked furiously and even Dineo helped by carrying fistfuls.

Rra Thopi was the first of the villagers who worked in Boomdal to return, riding his new bicycle.

"What's this?" he called out.

"Do your eyes not see?" replied Rra Rampou. Naledi was close to him and could hear the old man's short, panting breath. His tone was curt. Perhaps he too was wary of Rra Thopi.

With darkness falling, it was decided that whoever was able would continue the work the next day. Already a good number of stones had been sorted out into piles according to size and a lot of thatch had been cleared.

As they left to go home they heard Mma Tshadi calling to them. Straining her eyes, Naledi could just make out the shapes of two people coming towards them along the Boomdal track. Mma Tshadi and Taolo were returning from their visit to the magistrate. They must have realised something was wrong because even from a distance Mma Tshadi was exclaiming in horror.

"What have they done now, those devils?"

Nor was their news any better. The magistrate had kept them waiting the whole day before agreeing to see them. There had been nowhere to sit and they had been left standing in the corridor since the waiting room was for 'Whites Only'. Finally they had been allowed into his room. The clerk made it clear how privileged they were to see him without an appointment. The magistrate continued writing at his desk for a time before looking up at them, irritation written on his face. Although there were seats, they were left standing while he remained seated. He asked Mma Tshadi brusquely why she was bothering him when 'everything should be quite clear by now to you people'. When she asked for his reply to the villagers' request that Saul Dikobe represent them, the magistrate lost his temper. Banging the table with his fist, he thundered at them that Chief Sekete was still their chief – and would remain so until he died, and the sooner they all went to join him in Bop, the better. Then he had issued a warning to Taolo, saying he knew all about his activities and how foolish he was to follow in his father's footsteps. Without allowing them any discussion, the magistrate then rang for his clerk to show them out like two naughty children.

An icy chill spread inside Naledi as she listened. For once, Mma Tshadi's normally strong voice had lost its firm edge. Taolo did not speak. It was unusual for him to be so quiet. Naledi could not see his face in the dark, but she could feel the tension in his body.

Mma Tshadi's account shocked everyone. They had beaten back their despair at the ruin of their church by sorting and hauling the stones to rebuild it. But the magistrate's callous words now thrust deeper into their wounds. How could they win against such an enemy?

"What can we do?" The speaker voiced everyone's feelings.

"My friends, it's not finished yet! We must be prepared for a long struggle." It was Mma Dikobe's voice. She must have arrived while Mma Tshadi was speaking: "Why should you be surprised at the magistrate? Has he not always behaved in this way to you? Should we give up now because of this man? No . . . we have a plan. Already we are busy with a letter to the Minister as our friends from the Removal Committee advised. We'll tell him we are being forced out against our wishes and he said no-one is to be forced."

Her voice was soft, yet clear. She paused, but there were no interruptions:

"He too will ignore our letter unless he sees that many people are watching him. So we will ask our friends to give a copy of our letter to the newspapers. They can photograph our ruined church and send these pictures all around the country, even to other countries. But we must speak with *one* voice. If some of us give in, then they will break us off one by one, like the branches of a dead tree.'

There was a hum of approval and Mma Tshadi summed it up:

"Sister, you give us courage," she said simply.

Out of the surrounding darkness, the jagged church walls began to emerge in outline as the bright round disc of the moon rose into the night sky. Before leaving, it was agreed to hold a meeting the following evening to approve the letter to the Minister. They would also elect their own Village Committee to represent them in the trouble ahead, no matter what the magistrate had said. Why should they let their enemy decide their future?

CHAPTER 24

At home Naledi hurried to prepare some of the mealie meal Nono had bought after collecting her pension money. The shop prices in Bop had been even higher than in Boomdal. Speaking to local customers, the villagers were told that most of the shops were owned by people who were friendly to those in high places. It seemed that to get on in that place you not only had to be Tswana, you had to belong to the President's party.

It was late when they finished eating. Usually by this time they would be fast asleep. But when Naledi asked Nono if she could go for a short while to Mma Dikobe's to see how the letter was coming on, her grandmother did not object. Was Nono just too worn out to worry any longer or was this another sign of a change of heart? Her wrinkled eye-lids closing, she even nodded when Tiro announced that he would go as well.

Lamps and candles had already been extinguished in most of the houses and the sound of their softly thudding feet and gasps for breath were amplified by the quiet. They noticed a light still flickering in one of Rra Thopi's rooms. Once at the top they saw that the Dikobe household was also still lit up. No wonder Mma Dikobe was suspicious of Rra Thopi. His was the only house in the village from which the Dikobes could be seen. In fact one of his windows faced their house. Glancing at it, Naledi thought she saw a movement at the curtain.

Outside the Dikobe's door they could hear muffled voices which became silent immediately they knocked. Tapping again, Naledi called softly.

"It's only us!"

The door opened and an anxious Mma Dikobe quickly ushered them inside.

"What a fright you gave us! It's so late. We thought . . ."

"No, Mma! The police don't knock so politely. They'd have broken the door down by now!" Taolo intervened.

He was sitting at the table with Mma Tshadi and Rra Rampou. There was a seat for Mma Dikobe and an extra one pushed aside, as if someone else had got up in a hurry.

"We came to see about the letter," Tiro said in his young resolute voice.

With one of her rare slow smiles, Mma Tshadi slipped her hand down the front of her dress and produced a folded piece of paper. Smoothing it out, she placed it on the table.

At the same time a door opened behind her and Saul Dikobe came in. He was imposingly tall.

"So two young activists! That's good. We can do with your fresh brains!"

"Please, Saul, why don't you stay in the other room?"

There was no hiding Mma Dikobe's worried tone.

"We can still talk across to you in there. If the police break in, at least they won't see you with us."

But her husband simply shook his head as he sat down at the table.

"Look Lydia, if they want to take me, they'll take me. We're just too short of time to play their games. We must have the letter finished tonight. Let's continue now. It's almost done."

He spoke quietly but with an authority which would have been hard to contradict. It was difficult to imagine how a man with such dignity would look as a closely-shaven prisoner, having to jump to the orders of prison guards, thought Naledi.

"I can keep a look out for you, Mma!" Tiro offered.

Slipping past Mma Tshadi's chair to the window, he put his left eye to the window frame, barely shifting the curtain. Over the past few weeks, her brother had altered. He talked less and his voice had developed a hard edge except, Naledi had noticed, when he was speaking to Mma Dikobe. Only when she was around did something emerge of his old self. Did she remind him of their own Mma so far away?

Rra Dikobe passed Naledi the letter.

"Read it aloud to us," he said. "Then we can all hear how it sounds."

Naledi looked down at the lines of neatly curving script, written in English. She could tell it was not the final copy because there was the occasional crossing out and correction.

MEMORANDUM TO THE MINISTER OF
CO-OPERATION AND DEVELOPMENT

FROM THE PEOPLE OF BOPHELONG

INTRODUCTION

Sir, we have heard that a statement has been made that there will be no more forced removals. Only those who want to go will be moved. So we wish to bring to your urgent attention our position.

Bophelong is freehold land that has been owned by members of the Sekete family since 1910. A Deed of Transfer showing this transaction is held by Mr Elias Sekete who was our Chief until he deserted us nearly four weeks ago. The farm was bought before the law was passed forbidding black people to own land here. Many of our families have been tenants of the Seketes for a very long time. In fact some of these families were already living together in this place before 1910 and the oldest male member of the Sekete family has traditionally been the chief of this community. Now we find a terrible thing has happened without any consultation with us. We find that Elias Sekete who was our Chief has agreed for all of us to move into the place called

Bophuthatswana. When the truth came out and he saw how angry the people were, he ran away. Because he deceived us and did not consult with us over such an important matter in the customary way, we do not believe he can represent us any more. This is why we are appointing a Bophelong Village Committee to speak with one voice on our behalf.

GRAVES

Our ancestors have lived in this place for a long time. Their bones are buried here and their graves are sacred to us. We must remain here to protect them from being ploughed up and treated with disrespect.

LAND, CROPS AND LIVESTOCK

Even as tenants many of us have our own plots for growing crops such as maize, beans, cabbages etc. We are not self-supporting but this land adds to our income and has helped to keep some residents from starvation in hard times. There is also no shortage of common land here for grazing our cattle and tenants who can afford it keep goats, pigs and poultry.

We hear that in Bophuthatswana only the landowners will receive land for growing and grazing. As tenants we will not be entitled to any land. What would happen then to our cattle? How will we manage without them and without land?

IMPROVEMENTS

Over the years we have constructed many wattle and daub huts as well as a fine stone building for our church. This week, without any warning, our church was destroyed by men in government trucks. We have put up fencing, cattle kraals, pit toilets and a cattle dipping tank. After the river was dammed up causing us to lose our source of water, we contributed to the cost of laying pipes so water is now brought to a tap in our village. We pay the white farmer for use of this water. You can see from this that we have made many improvements to the land.

SCHOOLS
Children with parents who can afford the fees walk daily to school in Boomdal where there is a Primary and Secondary school. Our community donated funds to help build these two schools.

EMPLOYMENT
Many of our younger people are working in town or away from the district but other women and girls can get casual work on neighbouring farms. In Bophuthatswana the only work available is far away and transport costs are high.

CONCLUSION – REJECTION OF REMOVAL
The tenants of Bophelong are totally opposed to this removal. It would result in:

(a) Misery and hardship with heavy losses of property.
(b) Disruption of lives and . . .

Naledi's voice came to a halt where the letter stopped. She was pleased she had managed even the longer English words, in spite of small hesitations.

"What do you think of it?" asked Rra Dikobe. Naledi felt them all looking at her, waiting for her opinion. It was a good letter, direct and to the point, but . . .

"Well child?" Mma Tshadi urged.

"It's all true what you write, but why should this Minister listen? It's *his* people that want to force us away!"

"That's why we don't send it only to him. We make copies and get it published to bring it all in the open as quickly as possible." Taolo's voice was impatient.

"If we embarrass them, they might hold off for a while," put in his father. "But, there's truth in the girl's question. People listen to you when you are strong, not when you are weak. That's why poor people like us need to join together to become like a chain so together we can be strong. At the moment we're still weak and if they choose, they can smash us tomorrow. Their machine is waiting," he added quietly.

"Then let them do it. Let them leave my bones here too. They can shoot me but they won't take me!" Rra Rampou shook his cropped grey head vigorously.

Mma Dikobe reminded them that the letter had still to be finished. Naledi and Taolo argued successfully that the letter should mention the police raid, as well as Boomdal and the attack on the students there. Although Tiro had his back to the group throughout the discussion, with his eye to the window, Naledi was sure he was following everything. Every now and again his shoulders would twitch, his body taut and tense. Mma Dikobe must have noticed too, because as they were preparing to leave she gently rubbed her hand over Tiro's shoulders.

"You children need some rest," she said.

A light was still flickering in the far room of Rra Thopi's house. As they passed by, Naledi carried with her not only Rra Dikobe's words about the need to become strong like a chain, but the uneasy fear that lurks in shadows.

CHAPTER 25

The morning light was cutting sharply through slits in the curtains when Naledi and Tiro were woken by a loud knocking at the door. Struggling up from her mat, Naledi pulled on her dress. Although awake, Nono still lay in bed, clearly not recovered from the previous day's journey.

Outside were two of the Sadire children with the news that no water was coming from the tap. What should they do? Their little brother was not well and their mother had left them with instructions to see that he kept drinking. She had not been able to stay at home herself because the farmer for whom she worked would dismiss her if she didn't go to work. Naledi checked the supply in their own bucket. It was very low, but by tipping the container to one side she was able to scoop out a cupful of water which she handed to the older child.

Tiro and Dineo set off at a run towards the tap. As Naledi approached, she could see Mma Tshadi and Taolo among the small crowd. People were dismayed, disbelieving. Why should the water stop so suddenly? Every month their chief used to collect money from each family to pay to the white farmer who owned the dam. No one knew what had happened since Rra Sekete had deserted them, but surely the farmer would not just cut them off? Why hadn't he sent someone to the village to ask for the money if that was the problem?

Someone would have to go to the farmer to find out the reason. Someone else could begin going round to collect the dues and those away at work would be asked for their contribution at the meeting planned for that evening.

It was quite a distance to the farm otherwise Mma Tshadi said she would have gone to question the farmer herself. So she asked Taolo and Naledi to hurry over there. Seeing Tiro set to follow, Mma Tshadi called him back. His eyes and lips hardened, but relaxed when he was told that he was needed to help collect the water money.

Taolo and Naledi cut across the grazing veld behind the Dikobe's house. It was the opposite direction to Boomdal and there was no path. The quickest way to the dam was simply to follow the line of piping which carried the water to the village tap. Usually if you put your hand on the pipe you could feel its vibrations. To-day it was still. Crossing a small donga, patches of dry red earth protruding through the grey grass, Taolo put out his hand to help Naledi up the far side. He held on to it as they half jogged, half walked. The rounded wall of the concrete dam was visible now, partly shaded by a row of tall and stately blue-gum trees. At either side of the dam behind wire fencing were the varied greens of well-watered crops, the tell-tale sign of a white-owned farm.

The slight pressure of Taolo's hand was comforting, in contrast to the tight knot Naledi felt inside her as they approached the place. Perhaps it was the same for Taolo too, in spite of his usual calm air. It was possible to slip through the fence at this point, but unwise. Better to walk the longer way round to the gate.

Walking alongside the farm's boundary, a voice brought them to a halt. Coming up behind them from the direction of the dam, was a man wearing a khaki brown shirt, trousers and hat. His manner was not unfriendly, but he wanted to know what the young people were doing so close to the farm. He was the 'boss-boy', the white farmer's foreman, and he had to report to the farmer on all comings and goings.

"We are from Bophelong, Rra. There's no water," Naledi told him.

"People want to know what's happened so we've come to see the farmer," Taolo added directly.

The man shook his head, sucking air through his teeth. It was a bad thing he said, but the water had indeed been cut off late the previous evening, following a visit from the police. Police and soldiers came to the farm frequently these days. It was all this business of what they called 'terrorists'. His own job was becoming more difficult by the day.

"Every time the police come, then I must check this,

check that. It's too much now."

"But why did the farmer stop our water?"

Impatience was overcoming Naledi. What did the police visits have to do with their water?

"The police say the terrorists are in your village. That's why they told my boss he must stop the water."

Suddenly it was quite clear. It was not the money at all. First the church was wrecked. Now the water. The farmer was simply helping the authorities force them away. He would not reconnect the water even if they paid the money. It seemed there was nothing they could do. Controlling his anger and trying to seem casual, Taolo asked how the water was actually turned off. But the foreman immediately became suspicious, warning them that he'd overheard talk about soldiers being posted on the farm.

The journey back felt much longer. They were both hot and thirsty. The attack was coming from all sides. How would they manage without the tap? By carrying buckets all the way on foot from Boomdal? Or would it be possible to get some large barrels filled with water in Boomdal, and find someone to drive once or twice a day with them over to Bophelong?

As they came in sight of Taolo's house they spotted a grey landrover. From the distance, it looked like a toy car. It was bumping over the slope past Rra Thopi's, coming to a stop outside the Dikobe house. A group of figures could be seen jumping out of the back and running up the path. Then they were out of sight.

With a shout, Taolo streaked forward. Racing after him, Naledi yelled, "Wait Taolo! Maybe it's you they're looking for!"

But he didn't slow down until they saw the figures returning to the landrover and jumping into the back unaccompanied. They were close enough now to see that a couple of them wore caps which looked like army peaked caps, although the rest of their clothing was ordinary. Two other men were in the front of the vehicle, one of them looking through binoculars. Taolo and Naledi were now too close to hide. The men in front were white, those behind black. With a sudden surge the landrover swerved off the path and onto the veld. It was heading straight towards them.

There was nowhere to go. Naledi gripped Taolo's arm, pulling him towards a thorn bush, but it was pointless. In no time at all the machine had careered at speed across the uneven earth right up to them, slowing down to let four large men jump out from under the canvas and pounce on Taolo. As he tried to fight loose, Naledi pulled desperately at one of the men holding him. Suddenly an elbow hit her fiercely in the stomach. Winded, she doubled over onto the ground. Through sharp spasms of pain, she was aware of Taolo being dragged into the back of the landrover. Mingled with the roaring of the vehicle as it recklessly ploughed its way over the village pasture, was a long, bitter scream.

CHAPTER 26

Naledi was still trying to get control of her breath and push herself up from the ground when Rra Dikobe reached her. He had seen it all from on top. The moment the four men had rushed into the house, pushing him aside, he had known they were after Taolo. But there had been no way to warn him. Everything had happened so quickly.

Rra Dikobe spoke more rapidly than usual, but his voice was very quiet. His eyes were deeply worried.

"They could take him anywhere and there's almost nothing we can do. They're from the army I'm sure of it, but we have no proof. I should have looked at the number-plate. They were so fast."

Putting his hands to his face, he pressed the palms over his eyes and forehead.

Should she go to the hospital and tell Mma Dikobe? Naledi felt there must be something she could do. But Rra Dikobe said she must find Rev Radebe first. If he collected Mma Dikobe in his car, together they might be able to start some sort of search. It was very possible the men would beat Taolo up in some remote place for their own amusement and then let him go. As he said this, Naledi felt Rra Dikobe was holding back much greater fears. She quickly told him of the conversation at the farm, then hurried off to find Mma Tshadi. Water had also to be brought from Boomdal as soon as possible. They would need Rev Radebe's help in both matters.

When he had collected whatever water dues he could, Tiro went with Naledi to Boomdal. Mma Tshadi had made him responsible for the money. He counted it carefully before tying it into a piece of cloth which he tucked deep into his trouser pocket.

It took them over an hour to find Rev Radebe in Boomdal. It was his day for visiting parishioners and that meant tracking him down. Naledi's anxiety grew in leaps and bounds but once found, Rev Radebe rapidly moved into action in his old blue Ford. Within a short time he not only got them six large barrels of water, but he also persuaded one of his parishioners to make a journey in his van to Bophelong, charging only for the petrol. The man agreed to make the delivery, offering to take the two young people back with him. Rev Radebe made light of the difficulties of making a daily arrangement telling them to leave it to him. Shocked to hear of Taolo's abduction and of the destruction of the church, he promised to collect Mma Dikobe from the hospital and together they would conduct an immediate search of the area for Taolo in his car.

As the van bumped noisily along the track, it seemed to Naledi that they were now continually at the edge of a sharp blade. The authorities were chopping at them from all sides and yet they were managing to hold on to the threads of life. They were being worn down, being forced to struggle for every basic thing, but somehow they were still together. But where would they be without friends in Boomdal? For how long could they exist without water? At tonight's meeting, they must discuss how to work closely with the Boomdal Resistance Committee.

The roar of the engine mingled with painful echoes of Taolo's scream. What state was he in now? It only took seconds for lives to be broken, for the threads to snap.

Shouts and praises greeted the van as it pulled up past the bulldozer by the church-yard where a number of villagers, Mma Tshadi included, were busy at work. In minutes a queue had formed behind it, with Naledi and Tiro, each with a bucket, dipping in and pouring the precious water into one container after another. When the queue ended, Mma Tshadi asked the driver if the remaining two full barrels could be left in her house for those at work who would return to the village later. Could he possibly find a further couple of barrels so they could receive another six full barrels the next day? Naledi marvelled at Mma Tshadi's directness. People rarely refused her requests unless they were like the white magistrate.

*

The sky to the west spread out in layers of deepening pink as villagers assembled that evening beside the piles of stones in the church-yard. Some stood, some sat on the ground and a few on benches which had been salvaged from the wreckage, Nono among them. She insisted on coming, although she needed to lean heavily on Naledi during a slow walk from their house. A table and a chair had been produced from somewhere, borrowed from someone's house. The church table had been smashed during the bulldozing, its remains already chopped up for firewood.

Everyone knew about the attack on Taolo. Mma Dikobe had been due to come to the meeting with the letter for the Minister. As the sky's pink turned to purple, the villagers waited patiently but with growing apprehension as they listened for the sound of Rev Radebe's car. Naledi had to keep fighting off an image of a figure lying sprawled out, motionless, hidden in long grass. She wondered what Taolo's father must be going through, imprisoned and alone in his house. At the same time her eyes silently followed the movements of Rra Thopi. For a while he stood near Mma Tshadi and Rra Rampou. Now he moved to the back of the gathering quite close to where she stood. Every now and again, she was aware of him glancing sideways, over in the direction of Boomdal.

At last a pair of car-lights appeared over the western slope. The shape was that of the old Ford. Rev Radebe and Mma Dikobe must have approached the village from the west and already stopped at the Dikobe house. Naledi bit her lip. If only . . . But as the two figures approached the lamp-light, it was obvious they had not found Taolo. After a few whispered words, Mma Tshadi announced that Rev Radebe would begin the meeting with a prayer.

"Ditsala tsame, my friends, while we are gathered this evening, in this place which others have desecrated, another one of our children is missing . . ."

He began softly, but slowly and steadily the pitch of his voice began to rise. When it could go no higher, it would drop suddenly again before its next ascent. Naledi felt her heart rise and drop with his words. It was like their struggle. On and on, drop, on and on, drop, on and on, yes, always, on and on, in spite of the times you dropped back.

The prayer was over and discussion turned to the reason for the meeting. Mma Dikobe was asked if she would prefer someone else to read the letter, but she replied clearly,

"No, I'll do it."

The pain was there in her voice, but she was refusing to give in to it. Sitting at the table, reading by the light of the paraffin lamp, she spoke the words with the steadiness of someone planting a line of strong stakes in the ground. Only at the word 'Children' did her voice waiver slightly. When she came to the end of the letter and the final words, 'For these reasons, we are not prepared to move', there was a momentary silence and then applause.

Mma Tshadi rose from the shadows of the front row and moved up to the table, the strong square features of her face lit up by the lamp.

"If anyone wishes to say something about the letter, please say it now."

There was shuffling as someone stood.

"You have put our whole story there very truly, but why . . ."

The speaker stopped midway. A figure was stumbling down the track towards them . . . No, it was two figures, one supporting the other.

Shocked cries greeted Saul Dikobe as he staggered into the ring of light carrying the boy's weight on his shoulder. Mma Dikobe and those in front rushed to help him. Rev Radebe raised his voice.

"Bring him to the car. Let me take him to hospital."

"Nyaa-a-a! . . . first . . . the meeting!" Taolo's strangled words cut across the gathering.

"He insisted I brought him here . . . crawled back

from where they left him . . . wouldn't stay at home . . ."

Rra Dikobe was short of breath. Carefully he lowered Taolo to the chair, while his mother anxiously bent over him. Naledi squeezed through people to get to the front. The right side of Taolo's face was swollen and cut, his right eye almost closed. Leaning forward, his arms clasped his stomach tightly, one hand clenching a dark-stained handkerchief. He nodded when his mother asked if he'd been hit in the stomach, but her pleas with him to go with Rev Radebe were in vain. He would not go to the hospital until after the meeting.

It was Tiro who noticed Rra Thopi slipping away. The moon had come out and the shadowy figure hurrying quietly away behind the broken wall was unmistakeable. Tiro tugged at Mma Tshadi to get her attention. Within seconds the message had been passed on and Mma Dikobe was urging her husband to leave the gathering. Rra Thopi's disappearance could mean only one thing.

"Please Saul, don't let them find you here."

Everyone was quiet, all eyes focussed on the family around the table. The flickering orange and blue flame of the lamp lit up sections of each face, and Saul Dikobe's had become set and resolute.

"No! They are *not* going to make me run like a frightened dog! They are *not* going to make me desert my son so they can attack him all over again! No, they are *not* going to stop me from talking here tonight! Will they destroy me, my family, my people while I must sit quietly by and watch? Oh no!"

His deep voice rang out across his moon-lit audience, the surrounding rubble and debris, and into the darker recesses beyond. Perhaps Rra Thopi could hear him too . . . or whoever was lurking there. Naledi felt the whole world could have been listening and Saul Dikobe would still have spoken the exact same words. Nothing would make him alter the truth. He spoke of those with power who used it to break the weak, of the white authorities pushing them off their land into the barren, bottomless pit of a labour reserve.

"Once in Bop, the only way out will be if they need you to work. Otherwise they will leave you to rot."

He spoke of corruption and greed, of those from their own community who helped the authorities just for their own gain, but they would not be safe from the people's anger. It would spill over against those who betrayed them. Had their own chief's house not been set on fire?

And then he began to speak of resistance, especially of the spirit of young people who were saying 'No' when their parents were waivering, who said suffering was nothing new, but this time they were determined to fight it out to the end. Many times in the past people had joined together to resist the unjust laws. They had formed unions. They had formed congresses. Almost thirty years ago, as a young man in his early twenties, he had made his way to a place called Kliptown where people from all across the country, from all backgrounds, had come to agree on a Freedom Charter. That day they had committed themselves to struggle. Although the government kept trying to crush and destroy them, it could never put out the fire in people's hearts, their burning desire for freedom.

He continued speaking even when the headlights appeared from the direction of Boomdal, two sets of them.

"You must elect your committee. When the police come for some of them, you'll find new people to take their places, old and young."

"Please Rra, please go now! There's time!"

The headlights were getting closer and Tiro could not contain himself. Rra Dikobe looked calm.

"No, my child, if they were coming for you, I'd tell you to run. Then you could fight them later. But tonight, I'm not running."

Naledi watched the harsh white beams as they spilt

over the dark veld, rapidly approaching their own dim yellow circle. It was hard to accept, but perhaps Rra Dikobe was right. He was in a trap already and he was refusing to behave like a frantic animal. When the two vehicles jerked to a halt right beside them, with the headlights glaring directly onto the gathering, Saul Dikobe was still speaking. He carried on even as doors rattled and uniformed men jumped out flashing torches. Taolo tensed, sitting upright, his arms still gripping his stomach. His mother moved closer to him.

"Saul Dikobe!" barked a voice.

Slowly Rra Dikobe turned his head towards the mass of spreading lights, narrowing his eyes against the glare.

"So, we have caught you red-handed! You had better tell your little gathering to disperse. This meeting is illegal. The Chief hasn't asked permission from the magistrate."

No one moved. The voice spoke in English. Another one followed, this time in Tswana.

"Phatlang! . . . Break up! Go to your homes! This meeting is illegal!"

Rev Radebe was the first to respond, moving towards the first voice.

"I'm a priest. Let me talk to the one in charge."

"There's nothing to discuss. Everyone must go home . . . except Saul Dikobe. He's coming with us."

With that, bodies and torches suddenly lunged forward towards Saul. Naledi heard Taolo shout.

"Leave him!"

There was an ear-splitting crack and screams . . .

"Oh God! Oh God! They've killed him!"

Mma Dikobe's voice was heaving in great gasps. Horrified, people drew back from the echo of the gun. The lamp was knocked off the table and shattered. The yellow circle was replaced by the searing white cones of the head lights cutting through the dark. At the end of one of them lay the body of Saul Dikobe.

CHAPTER 27

It was a nightmare from which there was no escape. Lying on her mat Naledi tried to find relief in sleep but whichever way she tossed, the nightmare remained. Half-asleep, she was surrounded by bright lights, bursts of gun-fire, writhing bodies . . . each with a face she recognised. Half-awake she could not get away from the motionless shape on the ground, the heart-breaking gasps of, "They've killed him", and the dreadful scene that followed as Rev Radebe argued with the police over the body, trying to stop them hauling it away. He kept his voice low and steady while the police were loud-mouthed and jittery, shouting that everyone should go home. They were shoving people with their rifles, forcing them away from the old church-yard. Naledi could see Mma Kau supporting Nono, stopping her from being trampled underfoot. Children were screaming and Dineo was lost in the crush. Police were now forcing them back into the darkness beyond the trucks, shouting, "Go home!" Rev Radebe's pleas could be heard in between the shouts and cries. But they were of no use. The police insisted on taking the body for 'investigations'. The villagers watched the body lifted into the back of one of the vehicles and driven off towards Boomdal. Then Rev Radebe left, taking with him Mma Dikobe and Taolo, both silent with grief.

Naledi's mind replayed the scene again and again, as if desperately seeking a different ending. But each time it was the same. On one occasion the high-pitched screaming of the petrified children came closer and closer until she realised that Dineo was really screaming in the room next door, waking in the middle of a nightmare. Nono was trying to soothe her with her weak hands. But the child sensed her grandmother's frailty and it seemed to increase her terror. Hysterical, she clutched wildly to her elder sister as Naledi took her from Nono's bed.

Sitting by the table in the dark, softly stroking Dineo's hair and enclosing the little body in her arms, Naledi knew how unprotected her sister was. Tiro, at eleven, had his own kind of bitter defiance ready to spit out his hatred of those with power over them. Returning home that night his young face had been hard. Yet Naledi knew how much he had admired and respected Rra Dikobe. He had loved their own father so much, and had been distraught and inconsolable at his death, killed by the sickness from the white people's mines. But her brother had changed since then and now that guns had taken away Rra Dikobe, he was not going to let his pain show, perhaps not even to himself. It was too big.

Naledi's eyes were wet. She could not stop her tears. They were hot and angry. She wiped her hand across her face but drops still fell onto the child on her lap. She was meant to be reassuring Dineo and here she was weeping herself. There was a time, when she was younger, when Nono could have comforted them both. That time was gone. Nono used to say, "All will come right." But it wasn't true, not any more, if ever. Even if she weren't ill and worn out, Nono could not say it now. Perhaps that was the very reason she was not getting better. Their grandmother had given up believing that 'all will come right'.

Once, too, there was a time when Naledi would have longed for their mother. But she knew now that her mother had no power either to make things come right – and it hurt too much to think of her. There had been no further word since the letter saying the 'Madam' would not let her come.

Clasping Dineo, Naledi felt her way back to her mat. The child was no longer hysterical but her body was still shaking with sobs. Naledi lay her down and crept in beside her, unable to stop her own salty tears from running their course. Dineo's small hand reached for her sister's face, as if checking the source of the dampness. They gave each other the comfort of their bodies and slowly that warmth, together with the intense anger and grief which was burning inside her, helped dry Naledi's tears. You had to go on. Mma Dikobe and Taolo had to go on. Her friend Grace, whether she was in hiding or in prison, had to go on. Their own Mma had to go on. They all had to continue in their different ways. The alternative was to give up, as Nono seemed close to doing, but she was old, sick and exhausted and Naledi had no excuse like that. Dineo was breathing deeply, no longer awake. Naledi felt drained, but at last her mind blanked out and she too fell asleep.

They were woken by a terrible commotion. For a few seconds Naledi thought it was the nightmare again. It was still dark inside, but the noise was real. They were the same sounds as the evening before, the yelling and the shouting, but now with a new sound added. A voice was booming over a loudhailer, blurred at first, until through repetition the words sorted themselves out. They were being told to move! . . .

"Pack all your belongings. Stack them outside. Take down any parts of your house you want to go with you. Don't leave your yard without permission until you're told to load things onto the trucks."

Opening the door just enough to look outside, Naledi and Tiro saw flashlights scudding in all directions. Behind them was the grim outline of a row of trucks and buses. The noise was coming from the direction of Mma Tshadi's place. Her house was obscured from view, but soon a group of scuffling figures appeared heading towards the trucks. Someone was being forcibly dragged, prodded and pushed along the path. Even in total darkness Naledi could identify the victim. The police could control Mma Tshadi's body, but not her tongue. A rough voice ordered her to 'shut up' but she continued to roar her defiance. In a streak of torchlight Naledi thought she saw the glint of metal. Was Mma Tshadi handcuffed? Was she being taken to Bop or to prison?

Before they could make out in which of the vehicles Mma Tshadi was being taken, Naledi and Tiro spotted two or three shapes moving in their own direction. Banging the door shut, they bolted it. The room was in darkness but Dineo had now woken and was crying for Naledi.

From Nono's bed came a hoarse whisper, "Oh God! What now?"

A great hammering shook the door.

"Open up! Open up!"

Neither Naledi nor Tiro moved. Seconds later there was a shattering of glass and a beam of light swung around the room. Dineo was scrambling across the room, screaming, to get to her sister. More splintering glass, fragments flying everywhere and a head thrust in through the open window. The torch's glare caught Naledi right in the eyes.

"Why did you not open the door? Hurry up! We haven't got all day!"

Slowly Naledi pulled at the bolt. Two large men pushed inside. One of them let his torchlight linger briefly on Nono.

"Why are you not up, mosadi mogolo, old woman? Today it's moving day. You must get up and get everything ready."

When Nono made no reply, the policeman turned to Naledi and Tiro.

"What's wrong with her?"

"Our grandmother is sick. You can see for yourself. How can she get up?"

"You'll have to make the place ready yourselves then. If you don't put your things outside they'll be broken up with the house. Sick or not sick, everyone is moving from here today. Don't waste time. The trucks are waiting. We'll be back soon."

As they turned to go, the other policeman said irritably,

"The child had better stop crying. These screaming kids will drive us mad."

Swivelling his torch, he directed it at Dineo who was desperately grabbing at Naledi's arms.

"Shut up! Or we'll lock you in the bus until we're ready to go," he rasped at her.

With that the two men stalked out, heading for the Sadires next door. Naledi lifted up her sister's small throbbing body and her hand touched something wet and sticky on Dineo's leg. The flying glass had caught her.

After struggling to light the candle, Naledi set to cleaning the wound as best she could. Pulling a shirt from the chest of drawers, she quickly folded and tied it around the leg as a bandage. Her mind pounded relentlessly. What could they do? There was no time to think clearly or to plan. The attack had come and they were still unorganised and defenceless. If they did not take their furniture and other belongings out of the house for removal, everything would be smashed as the bulldozers moved in. They would be left with only the clothes they were wearing. There could be no doubt that the police were serious. The family did not have much, but whatever little there was had been worked for with sweat and pain.

Persuading Nono to remain lying down and placing Dineo beside her, Naledi said the bed could be moved last of all. Although Tiro had not uttered a word since the police had broken in, he grimly began to help Naledi shift things outside, the table and two chairs, the orange crates that served as stools, the chest of drawers. The children and Nono had been so excited when Mma had arrived one time from the station in a taxi with an open boot and the chest of drawers bulging out. The 'Madam' had been throwing it out, but Mma had taken it. They had all delighted in her humorous account of the trouble she had getting it onto the train in the crowded Jo'burg station. She had put it into the goods section and had been kept busy sticking her head out at every station on the way to check that no one else took it off the train! Their laughter had been that of relief and admiration, that in spite of all the obstacles, Mma had succeeded. Looking now at her brother's tight-lipped face as they heaved the chest of drawers over the door-step, Naledi wondered if he too remembered the happiness they had felt that day.

By the time dawn came, their possessions formed a small pile in front of the house. Next to their three-legged iron pot, a few smaller cooking items and plates stuck awkwardly out of the orange crates while other odds and ends including their clothes were wrapped in a blanket. Nono needed help to put on her old checked jacket and woollen hat before being led to a chair outside. Naledi and Tiro then struggled with the iron bed while Nono sat bent over, her head in her hands, Dineo clinging closely to her.

Across the village were similar scenes. The work of a life-time was reduced to a few bundles and a small pile of furniture. The still ripening mealies, the half-grown cabbages and sweet potatoes in the fields, all those would have to be left behind. What would happen to the livestock belonging to better-off villagers? Were they expected to leave this precious wealth behind? Intermingled with the crying of young children was the squawking of hens, trapped inside make-shift boxes. It seemed that only the animals and young children still had the energy to give voice to their protests. Everyone else now was grimly silent, the memory of yesterday evening a terrible reminder of the punishment to be meted out to those who refused to knuckle under.

The sound of hammering carried across from a house where someone was trying to dislodge the window frames. Those with corrugated iron roofs were dismantling them, Mma Kau included. Stretching up on a stool balanced against the wall of her house, she was shifting the large stones that held down her roof. Naledi looked at their own roof made of thatch. There was no way she or Tiro could take it down. Their father had always spent some time checking and repairing it on his rare visits home from the mines. Since his death, parts of the thatch had become straggly, although it still did not let in the rain. Rra had always been thorough, like his father before him, he said. His dream had been to build a house of stones when he had sufficient money. But it still would not have made any difference today. Rra Rampou's stone house was going to be knocked down as surely as those of branches and dried mud. It was all the same to their destroyers, now lounging by their vehicles waiting for the order to begin.

CHAPTER 28

As dawn turned to morning and the sun's fiery glow radiated into blue at the eastern end of the veld, the bulldozer began its onslaught. The villagers watched as the chain of command took effect. First, three white policemen climbed down from one of the trucks and a message was passed to the groups of black policemen relaxing in front of the vehicles. They straightened up, and two of them marched to a truck further back. They opened the door and a dozen or so black men in blue overalls jumped down. One jogged across to the bulldozer. It was these men who were to carry out the work under the sharp eyes and tongues of their police supervisors.

The noisy throttle of the bulldozer released a trigger among the waiting villagers. As the great hulking machine began its approach, they broke their silence and shouts rent the air.

"Shame on you!"

"Why don't you break your own houses!"

"God will punish you!"

But the machine still humped its way forward, the driver's face impassive. If he and the others who followed him on foot felt any shame or pity, if they were imagining their own homes, parents, wives and children being smashed down, they did not show it. But they did not look into the eyes of the distraught villagers. They had not developed the hard-eyed stares of their police masters.

Whose house would they destroy first? A policeman was pointing at Rra Rampou's stone cottage. The bulldozer lumbered towards the most admired dwelling in the village, the one over which Rra Rampou had sweated for years, slowly buying and placing a few more stones each month, determined to complete a home which could last for a hundred years.

"I want my children's children and their children to remember me!" he used to joke wryly.

The house, which he had finally completed hardly a year ago, was up the track beyond the church ruins. Although it was difficult to get a good view from Nono's yard, Naledi could see no sign of Rra Rampou. The door of the house, with its white-painted number, was closed and there seemed to be no pile of belongings outside. Mma Kau, whose house was a little nearer and who was still up on her stool, was also craning her neck to see what was going on.

"Rra Rampou must be inside! He hasn't brought anything out!" she shouted over to Naledi and her brother.

"He said he'll die here!" Tiro hissed the words.

"But they have to stop! Someone must get him out! He'll be crushed to death!"

Ignoring the loudhailer order, Naledi clambered over the yard wall and raced towards the bulldozer. It must be stopped! From behind she could faintly hear her name. Nono was anxiously calling her to come back. But her heart was beating fiercely, her blood pumping too angrily. She had to stop the monster machine, she *had* to! Other voices were now yelling at her, more vehemently, yet she ran blindly forward, almost reaching the bulldozer. Surely the driver would not push in the walls when he knew an old man was inside? Surely the driver in his blue overalls was not a murderer? She cried out to him.

"Stop Rra! You must stop . . ."

She flew headlong as someone tripped her up, an iron hand grasping her as she spun towards the ground.

"Did you not hear the order? Why are you not in your yard?" The policeman's thick fingers were crushing her arm.

"There's an old man . . . in the house . . . you can't break it . . . you'll kill him . . ."

Naledi could barely control her voice. Kill, kill . . . like you killed Saul Dikobe, reverberated in her brain.

"You think we're stupid? We know he'll run out when he sees the first bit of dust falling. Old people are full of talk! Now get back to your place. Your house is next!"

Roughly pushing her backwards, the policeman blocked her way forward. But the driver had stopped the bulldozer. He obviously understood her even though he spoke to the policeman in a language that was not Tswana. He now looked hesitant, unhappy about continuing while someone remained inside.

By now other policemen, including one of the white men, had come forward and a new plan was rapidly devised to flush out Rra Rampou. Unleashed by a signal, a bevy of them stormed towards the cottage, splitting into three groups as they approached. Some rushed the door, kicking and battering it with their rifle butts, while the rest tackled each of the side windows, smashing in the glass. With a revolver pointing into the room, the white officer was the first to climb through. Naledi's policeman joined the storming party, and she remained standing near the bulldozer, close enough to hear raised voices and swearing inside. Shortly afterwards the door swung open and the raiders marched out victorious, Rra Rampou wedged between them.

"This one's a skelm! You'll have to watch him. He had an axe in there!" declared the white officer.

Signalling to the workers in overalls, he ordered them to clear out the old man's belongings. They could have five minutes to throw everything outside before the bulldozer driver got to work.

"It's your own fault, old man, if your things get broken but you've already wasted our time. You should've cleared the house yourself. You're lucky I'm asking my boys to take this trouble over you, and you wanting to chop me with your axe!"

The voice twisted into mockery of the stooping, grey-haired, silent Rra Rampou. Naledi sensed the smoulderng hatred behind the glazed eyes of their village elder.

"We'll make sure someone keeps an eye on you all the way," continued the policeman and he nodded for the old man to be marched towards the trucks. The white man's gaze fell on Naledi but before he had time to speak, she turned and ran back to her own yard. There Nono had stopped Tiro from following her. The wrinkled bony hand was still holding on to Tiro's wrist. He could easily have pulled away but, aware of his grandmother's distress, he had stayed beside her. Dineo, sucking frantically at her thumb, had climbed onto Nono's lap. Naledi flung herself onto the ground next to them. There was nothing to do now except wait.

As Rra Rampou's thatch came tumbling down and the stones began to fall to the thundering sound of the bulldozer, the first of the white farmers arrived with their cattle-trucks. They had got wind of the removal and were coming to see what animals could be bought cheaply. Strolling over to the white policemen, they hardly bothered to glance at the bulldozer and the destruction of Rra Rampou's home. In spit of the distance and the noise, Naledi felt she could hear their casual chat.

Shortly afterwards another message came over the loudhailer:

"Only small livestock such as goats and pigs can be transported. If you still have cattle, you have a last chance to sell them now. Those who own cattle may leave their yards to come and talk with the farmers here."

Naledi immediately thought of Rra Thopi. He had kept one of the biggest herds but his cattle were all safely out of the way. So he was not among the dejected men and women who now came forward, reluctant and anxious. The farmers were offering rock-bottom prices and the villagers had to accept. What else could they do?

As Naledi watched the animals being brought out of their enclosures, the bulldozer began to make its way along the track in their direction. Behind it lay the wreckage of Rra Rampou's once neat stone cottage. Seeing the machine approaching them, Dineo buried her face in Nono's lap. Nono sat completely still except for her lips which moved silently over the words of a prayer. Close beside her, Tiro stood tensely. Naledi pushed her hand in to her mouth to stop her own impulse to rage and shout as the bulldozer hit the yard's mud wall. She and Tiro had helped Mma build that wall on one of her visits. Even Dineo, who could barely toddle then, had helped pat the wall flat, chattering and singing with them as they worked. Naledi watched the wall crack in a thousand places and crumble . . .

The driver fixed his eyes straight ahead of him, not looking at Nono, who was now staring at him through misted eyes. How could one person help break down another's home? What harm have I ever done you, her deeply-lined, mute face seemed to say. Gears grinding, the machine moved into position, edging towards the house. Two policemen stood casually behind it. Eyes fixed on the great thick blade of metal, Naledi watched it rise and smash into the earthern wall . . . rise and smash . . . rise and smash . . . With the engine roaring in her ears, she felt all her fury, hurt and pain rise up, with each movement of the machine. She had her own powerful blade . . . a red-hot blade of anger. Any tears that touched it now dried up immediately. It was ready, ready. Metal could only be matched with metal. You had to be as strong as metal. Something Taolo had said about being in prison flashed through her mind: "The more they try to crush you, the tougher it makes you."

Dry-eyed, Naledi watched their home reduced blow by blow to a pile of rubble, before the bulldozer moved on to its next target. As she and Tiro stepped into the wreckage, something caught her eye under the pile of tangled thatch and crumbled misshapen earthen blocks. Stooping down she pulled out – covered in dust but intact – Dineo's little doll Pula. Somehow forgotten in the panic, it had survived the battering. Dineo slid off Nono's lap and ran to Naledi. Clutching the doll tightly, her cheeks stained with tears, the child stared in bewilderment at the shattered remains of their home.

The bulldozer pushed its way onward across the village, flattening carefully tended vegetable patches, hedges, fences and walls, it mowed down whatever lay in its way. Slowly the lorries began filling up as people were forced, under the eyes of armed police, to load their goods with the help of the men in blue overalls. From time to time, a policeman would shout, 'Hurry up!' and the workers would then sling items up into the lorry, not caring whether they would be broken or not.

When their turn came, Naledi approached the man next to the lorry.

"Be careful with my grandmother's things. It's all she has."

Ignoring her completely, he grabbed a chair and slung it up to the person standing in the truck. There was a crack as it hit the lorry floor. Tiro rushed up and seized the second chair from the hands of the first man.

"My sister asked you to take care!" he shouted.

Roughly pulling the chair back out of the boy's hand, the man swore and pushed Tiro aside. The second chair flew up and came down with a crash. There was nothing they could do except stand by and watch until the last of their possessions had been loaded.

Nono sat wordlessly on the earth that had been her home since the time she had become a young married woman. Now, her skin loose and shrivelled, and her face etched with the hardships of a lifetime, she closed her eyes for she did not want to see any more. Naledi knelt down beside her, taking her hand. It felt cold, in spite of the midday heat. Her grandmother's energy seemed to be slipping away, here in the place where she had looked after and cared for her children and grandchildren.

"Please Nono, please don't give up now," Naledi whispered. "We'll come back, you'll see, we'll come back. It's not finished Nono, it's not finished . . ."

Nono opened her eyes to look at her granddaughter. Although she still did not say anything, Naledi felt the gaze at least acknowledged in some way what had been said.

The lorry had by now proceeded to Mma Kau's house. She was a little more successful in preventing her furniture from being hurled about. Firmly placing herself between the man on the ground and the lorry, Mma Kau took hold of every item and forced him to lift it more slowly. Perhaps he was reluctant to push a woman aside the way he had done Tiro.

When the truck was full, a policeman shouted across to Naledi that the family must come. Naledi and Tiro helped Nono up, supporting her one at each side as they walked, while Dineo clung to her sister's skirt. Pointing to the truck, the policeman signalled them to climb aboard. Mma Kau, the two removal workers and the children struggled to lift Nono onto the back of the lorry. Clearing some boxes off Mma Kau's mattress, Naledi made a place for Nono to lie down. The rest of them huddled into spaces along the side. Mma Kau's two hens squawked nervously from inside their makeshift cage.

Slowly the lorry shifted off, juddering heavily over the uneven track. All around they witnessed destruction, houses without roofs, doors and windows . . . broken walls . . . piles of rubble . . . trampled crops . . . Their lorry joined two others as they left the village. The one with Rra Rampou was being closely followed by a landrover with armed policemen.

As the road began to rise slightly Naledi was able to look back across the veld to the western end of the village and the Dikobe's white-washed house with its trees and neat vegetable patch. The bulldozer had not yet reached it, but it too would soon be laid waste.

They had failed to stop the move and had paid a terrible price. It was not possible to forget the awful injuries on the day of the student march, Theresa still lying in hospital hardly able to speak, the quiet David Sadire whose mother still did not know what the police had done to him, Taolo wrenched away from her and his piercing scream from the landrover, the deadly shot in the night and Saul Dikobe's body in a circle of yellow light. . .

But while these images flooded in, others could not

be kept out . . . of all the refusals to give in, Mma Tshadi, solid and defiant to the end, Rev Radebe, always ready to take risks for them, Zach, Dan, Ben and the friends who were still helping to hide them, Mma Dikobe, grief stricken but steadfast, Taolo and the iron look on his face, insisting that his father carry him to the meeting last night, Saul Dikobe and his words, "No! They are *not* going to make me run like a frightened dog!" She was reminded of other words, those which Taolo had spoken that night he had come out of prison and walked home with her, taking her hand:

"Those swines think they can break you. But it's the opposite. They can kill me, and lots of others, but we'll get what we want in the end, to live like free people."

Wedged in among the furniture with her family in a jerking, noisy government truck, Naledi knew the spirit of those words was burning deep inside her too.

CHAPTER 29

The heat was almost unbearable. Lying on her mat among their jumbled possessions the night of their arrival in the resettlement camp, Naledi tossed and turned. Even with the two windows wide open, the hot stale air remained trapped inside the small metal box, their new 'home'.

It had been late afternoon before they and their pile of belongings had been dumped outside a corrugated iron hut, simply one of hundreds set in long rows on the hard, dry earth of Matlapeng. The name suited it, 'place of stones'. For some families there were not even huts, only tents. Naledi recalled her dismay on first seeing the rows of identical grey-block houses when she and Tiro had been to Soweto. But this was much worse. Here it was in the middle of nowhere . . . and while Soweto had been teeming with life, this place seemed fit only for death. She had seen it immediately in the blown-out stomachs of children on the wayside and in the eyes of the people they had passed . . . eyes that spoke wordlessly of resentment and depression at witnessing the arrival of yet another convoy of broken furniture and lives.

Leaving them exhausted, parched and hungry, the empty truck finally rumbled away. Mma Kau was allocated the iron hut next to them. Although they had always been neighbours and within calling distance, there had previously been a stretch of veld between them. Now they were practically within whispering distance. Together they had helped each other, pulling things through each narrow door and preparing places to sleep for the night. With Tiro sent to find water and Naledi making a small fire outside over which to cook, Mma Kau had helped to settle Nono who lay listlessly, hardly speaking. For how much longer would she be like this? With Mma Dikobe no longer around, and the pills soon to run out, what could they do? The nearest hospital was likely to be even further than the Boomdal one had been from their village. And what about money to pay for treatment?

These questions continued to plague Naledi deep into the night. In this place it was going to be a struggle just to survive, let alone organise any resistance. Yet if they did not resist, they would surely end up with the same sunken eyes as some of those people they had passed on the way.

Two days later Joe arrived from the Anti-Removal Committee with a friend who worked on a newspaper. Rev Radebe had rung to tell him the bad news. Reaching the camp early in the morning, the two men were anxious to get away before their presence was reported to the police. Joe took photographs, of the bleak lines of huts without fields, of even veld, the rock hard landscape, the ploughshares and hoes lying idle. He photographed Mma Tshadi standing grimly outside her new shack and Rra Rampou leaning on his stick, his eyes fixed on the horizon in the direction of the home from which he had been wrenched. As people spoke, the reporter wrote busily in his notebook. Mma Tshadi insisted they would never stop demanding to be taken back to Bophelong. How were people meant to live here?

"Only God knows why He let us be taken from our land. But one day He will punish those who throw us, His children, around like stones," declaimed Rra Rampou.

"But we can't wait so long Rra. We must do something ourselves."

Naledi watched the reporter scrawl her words rapidly onto the page.

Then Joe and his friend were gone and they were left with the empty feeling of being completely cut off again. Only their anger prevented them slipping into despair and resignation. For that was what the government wanted. Only the fittest were meant to survive here. Only those with work outside this giant prison called a 'homeland' – and with money to pay the expensive bus fare – could leave. Yet even if Nono had been strong enough to manage the long bus trip back to the white farm, the fare would absorb most of her meagre pay. For any other jobs out of the area, like in the city, you had to get permission through the chief to leave. And that was just the first stage. Yes, Taolo had again been right when he said, "We are all handcuffed!" Being locked in jail could not be much different from being locked up outside.

No one was really surprised when it was discovered that Rra Thopi had not been moved along with them to the same camp. Rumour soon spread that he had been taken to the place where the Sekete family were settled, on the other side of some low hills scattered with thorn-bushes and rocky outcrops. Determined to see for themselves, Naledi and Tiro climbed the rough terrain one afternoon. The colour of the rocks reminded Naledi of their church back home. Could it have been from here that their forefathers had once carted stones to Bophelong? Reaching the top, they looked down on a valley with a few red-roofed, white-washed houses dotted among mielie fields, stretches of veld and clusters of trees. Sunlight glinted off water. Although the water level was fairly low, it was still a river and the surrounding land was as fertile as Bophelong had been before its river was dammed up by the white farmer. This was the price for which Chief Sekete and Rra Thopi had sold them!

Was Poleng down there or had her father sent her away to boarding school? Naledi had no wish to go any further. If the friend to whom she had once been so close wanted to see her, let her come over the hill, down into the barren slum where they had been dumped. Let her search among row upon row of iron huts and tents. It would be a first test – and if she didn't pass it by coming then what was that old friendship worth? Since the fatal day only a few weeks ago when numbers had been painted on their doors, their lives had suddenly parted. Naledi was forging friendships of a new kind, like strong, binding links in a chain welded in the fire of each of their hearts. In Boomdal there had been a man who did welding in his backyard and she always found it fascinating when she had stopped to watch. How was it that in the red heat of fire something soft and malleable could be turned into solid strength? Yet it happened. It was happening to her too. Even if Poleng came to find her, perhaps she would no longer have time for any friendships which did not stoke the same fire or help strengthen the chain which was now her only lifeline. It was up to Poleng to link on to the same chain – or leave her alone. Turning her back on the valley of farms and leaving Tiro to follow, Naledi began the descent to the camp.

Weak and almost totally dependent on Naledi and Tiro, Nono still asked them daily about school. Where was it? Had they found out the cost? Had they written to their mother? She checked over the same details incessantly, insisting their mother would somehow find the money. She avoided any references to the protests at Boomdal, clinging on to school as the only hope for her grandchildren. Naledi did not remind her grandmother that without her income from the farm work, there was less money than before. Nono was talking more and more about the past. In fact she seemed hardly able to take their new surroundings in properly.

There was a makeshift primary school at Matlapeng but no secondary school. For a long time the authorities had been promising to build a proper primary school, but in the meantime children were being taught in a building erected by the people themselves. It was made entirely out of sheets of corrugated iron with open holes for windows. Finding there was no fence when going to investigate, Naledi and Tiro went up close to peer through an open door. The dimly lit room inside was hazy with heat. A group of children were squashed together on benches, the rest crowded on the floor while a weary-looking teacher sat on the room's only chair next to a cracked blackboard.

"I'm not going there!" protested Tiro.

"Where else can you go?" asked Naledi.

It was not possible to see the secondary school. Students travelled to it by bus because it was in another area and too far to walk, so it would be necessary to have money for bus fare too. The school year was coming to an end and the new one would begin in a couple of months. Someone told Naledi that the students there had also been involved in protests. There had been some expulsions, followed by a short boycott and then more expulsions. Even in a remote place like this, the pot could boil over.

But before any decisions could be made about schooling, they needed to hear from Mma. Naledi wrote to her the day after their removal. Her reply would have to be collected from the post office in the general dealer's shop. It was one of a few old mud-walled buildings set amongst the iron huts, identifiable by a faded 'Drink Coca-Cola' notice stuck on its peeling door. Like the communal tap, it was a place for people to meet and talk. Every day, following the usual trip to collect water, Naledi walked between the rows of dwellings to the shop to ask if there was a letter for her.

After more than a week it came.

> 'I was praying this would not happen. I am sending you the newspaper where I got a shock to see all this horrible news. Then your letter came. I can't believe our home is gone. I hope to come and see you very soon.'

Mma's employer was planning to go away on holiday for two weeks over Christmas so she would come then. She enclosed a page from a newspaper with a picture of Rra Rampou standing outside an iron hut. Next to it was a report about the removal. Naledi looked at the headline: 'Black spot' removed: "They throw us around like stones". Slowly she read through the English words. Then her eyes slipped down to another smaller report below.

> **Fight for body continues**
> The wife of the dead trade union leader Saul Dikobe is still attempting to recover the body of her husband from

police custody. Mr Dikobe, a banned person, was shot dead earlier this week during a meeting to voice protests against plans to bulldoze homes and remove residents of Bophelong to the homeland Bophuthatswana. Mr Dikobe was banished to Bophelong earlier this year after completing a ten-year prison sentence on Robben Island.

It is thought that police may be holding back the body in order to prevent the funeral taking place in Soweto at the weekend when a large crowd would be expected to attend.

The report did not say where Mma Dikobe was, nor anything about Taolo, but it mentioned Soweto which had been the family's home until the banishment order. It was almost certain that Mma Dikobe and Taolo would return to living there unless there was a problem with accommodation or with the authorities.

Mingled with relief at hearing that Mama would be coming soon and disgust at the police refusal to hand over Rra Dikobe's body, Naledi felt a sharp stab of loneliness. She folded the paper as she stood in the full heat of the sun, looking across the landscape of dried earth and iron huts. She was missing Taolo so badly, more now than when he had been in prison. It was foolish to dream of how good it would be if they could be together. She missed his mother too. For the brief period in which she had got to know the Dikobes, it was as if Naledi had a mother within reach. But she could hardly wish that they be with her here in this desolate place. Instead they would have to remain linked by the chain.

Hurrying back with the news about their mother returning from Jo'burg for Christmas, Naledi wondered what Mma would say about her involvement in the protests. Would she try to warn Naledi off further trouble? Or would she give her support? Mma had never met the Dikobes but surely she would have warmed to them. Although not able exactly to put her finger on it, Naledi had begun to feel there was a subtle change even in Mma Kau who used simply to say everything was 'God's will'. It was not just the removal, thought Naledi. It had been since her son's disappearance after the Sekete fire and the suggestion that he was working secretly with freedom fighters. In spite of the police harassment and the nerve-wracking worry, the way Mma Kau spoke revealed a quiet pride in her son. There must be thousands of other parents like her. Would their own mother be like them too?

CHAPTER 30

Two weeks before Christmas Rev Radebe arrived unexpectedly. Word spread rapidly and an hour later he was conducting a short service in front of Mma Tshadi's hut. People crammed in between the metal dwellings to hear him.

Dineo clung onto Naledi's back, safe from the crush. As ever, Rev Radebe's words seemed to carry special meaning. Singing voices rose up in rich harmonies up above the stony ground and the corrugated iron, into the hot, still air. Naledi's mind wandered with the voices. Nono would be able to hear them from where she lay.

The preacher's words rang out:

"Christmas is a time of hope, especially for those who are suffering . . ."

Mma would be coming any day now, but this Christmas there would be no celebrations. She was going to be shocked to see Nono's condition. Mma Kau helped the children constantly but with their grandmother's energy slipping away slowly like precious drips of water from a cracked pot, the family's future seemed as bare and unknown as the cloudless sky above.

"Christmas is a time for renewing our deep bonds with each other . . ."

Chief Sekete had come over to the camp full of smiles and greetings, declaring his happiness to be back with 'his people'. He had been met with silence and terseness. Approaching Naledi, he had used his old fatherly tone, saying she should come and see Poleng before his daughter left for boarding school. Embarrassed and angry, Naledi had turned away. So Poleng was there, but she had not come.

"Christmas is a time for new beginnings. Children of Bophelong it is time for you to elect those who should represent you in your just struggle to return to your true homes."

Naledi's mind jerked out of its meanderings. Was Rev Radebe helping with another election? People were putting up their hands in support of Mma Tshadi, Rra Rampou and others. Then Mma Tshadi was proposing her, Naledi, as a youth member. Hands and voices proclaimed her elected too. Dineo was patting her on the head.

"What about Sekete?" a voice called out.

Heated words followed. Whatever he claimed, and whatever the authorities declared, they, the people of Bophelong, would reject him for ever. Instead, they chose Rra Rampou to be their new chief. He had suffered the same fate as the rest of them. He was the only one they would trust, along with the committee they now elected, to act on their behalf. A great wrong had been done them and they were determined to return to Bophelong.

The service-cum-meeting was over and the people were beginning to disperse when Tiro pulled at Naledi's arm.

"The Reverend is calling you!"

With Dineo still clinging to her back, Naledi made her way through to the front. Taking her by the arm, Rev Radebe led her a short way aside from the gathering.

"I have something for you. I promised specially to see this would reach you safely."

Searching with one hand in a pocket of his black gown, he pulled out an envelope.

"Mma Dikobe was in Boomdal a few days ago to collect the things I brought from their house. She wanted very much to see you and your family but there was no time. She had to get back to work. So I promised to convey her greetings to you and she entrusted me with this letter."

Giving her the envelope, Rev Radebe enclosed her hand with both his palms, pressing it firmly for a second.

"Mma Dikobe said she will miss you greatly, but will try to keep in touch. She's going to help the Anti-Removal Committee in her spare time. They are planning a special campaign on Bophelong."

Naledi's heart was beating fast. There was so much she wanted to know. Perhaps it would be in the letter. She would like to be able to talk more to Rev Radebe, but this was not the time, so she simply thanked him as he let go her hand.

"By the way, will you show me your house after I'm finished here? I want to see your grandmother. Mma Dikobe told me about her illness."

With a playful ruffle of Dineo's head, he turned and made his way back to his congregation. Dineo immediately clambered down from her sister's back to run after him.

Wanting to read her letter undisturbed, Naledi walked away in the opposite direction. In Bophelong she could easily have found a quiet stretch of veld. Or she could have taken the letter to her favourite childhood place down by the dry river-bed to read in the shade of the overhanging trees. But here there were only iron huts. There was no point searching for anywhere different. With the villagers' voices still audible, she stopped in the middle of the rutted track. Tearing open the envelope, she first pulled out a photograph cut out from a newspaper. It showed an enormous crowd of marching people, some with banners, although she could not make out the writing. Opening the letter, her eyes skimmed to the bottom of the page. It was not from Mma Dikobe after all. The signature said 'Taolo'.

Dear Sis Naledi,
So much has been happening that I haven't had time to write. We heard that you were forced to move the day after Rra was killed. Please write and tell me how it is where you are. You can get my address from the friend who brings you this letter.

We had a hard time getting my father's body. We wanted to bury him on the Sunday but the cops were worried about a big funeral so they stalled for time. In the end they gave us the body on the Monday. We made the funeral on Wednesday and there was still a massive crowd – thousands of them. The unions made a call and people just took off work. There were banners saying things like 'APARTHEID KILLS – KILL APARTHEID' and 'STOP KILLING OUR COMRADES'. One group had banners with dozens and dozens of names – all of people killed by the police. But people weren't crying. They were angry, shouting and singing. Some were even making the freedom shout 'Amandla' right in front of the tanks. Then others took it up and you could hear it going through the whole crowd. If the sky had a lid, I reckon it would have shifted from all our voices.

You should have seen how the cops turned out in force and did their usual stunts with tear gas to stop people getting to the cemetery to hear the speeches. They tried to say it was only for the family. But people just kept coming. However we think the cops had orders not to shoot because there were so many TV cameras from overseas and reporters asking us questions. I'm sure they'll soon be banning all these cameras so they can carry out their terror in private.

Our lawyer is now pressing for an inquiry. If we get one then we'll bring all the stinking rot out into the open. My hunch is that the guys who beat me up are the same criminals who shot Rra.

We are living back in Soweto with my father's brother. Perhaps the police are going to make problems for us but in the meantime Mma has got back her old job in Bara Hospital. She sends you warmest greetings.

There are big upheavals in schools here. Many students have been boycotting for months and haven't written their exams. In some schools armed soldiers are on patrol, even in the classrooms. We don't know yet what the position will be when the next school year starts after the Christmas holidays. We need to get education but how is it possible like this? Students and parents are going to meet soon to discuss it all and decide what to do.

By the way, I've heard people mention the name of the friend you had here in Soweto. If it's the same person, she's still locked up. they've got hundreds of us inside, just 'detained', no trials. Someone called prison the 'College of Politics' so now we talk here about going to 'University'!

Like my father always said, freedom lies at the end

of a long road and it's going to be a long struggle. Keep strong, Sis. I know you will.

Amandla!
Taolo.

Naledi's heart burnt. It was a fierce fire within her, as fierce as the sun bearing down on her now, forever welding new links in a chain . . . invisible but strong, binding her to people right here in this barren place as well as to Taolo, to her imprisoned friend Grace and to so many others. Each day the chain was lengthening, strengthening. She was not alone. They were not alone.

Staring again at the picture from the newspaper of thousands of defiant people at Saul Dikobe's funeral, Naledi felt herself in there with them, their faces merging in among those who had been crammed between the iron huts only a short while ago. She too had heard Rra Dikobe talk of 'the struggle' – and of sharing it. At first they had only been words to her. Now they were real.

She must show the picture and read Taolo's letter to others. Let them also feel the strength of the chain. Even Nono, sinking so fast, couldn't she feel it a little? A hum of voices was still coming from outside Mma Tshadi's hut. Letter and picture in hand, Naledi quickened her pace towards the gathering.

Bess

Robert Leeson

Bess Morten's flight from her overbearing guardian leads her to the New World in search of her brother Matthew. Determined and spirited, Bess has to fight for her right to independence, love, and to achieve the future she believes in.

This is an excellent adventure story and a sequel to *'Maroon Boy*.

Bess is a character that 'ought to place her high among the fictional heroines with readers of today'.
British Book News

All these books are available at your local bookshop or newsagent, or can be ordered from the publishers.

To order direct from the publishers just tick the titles you want and fill in the form below:

Name ______________________________

Address ______________________________

____

Send to: Collins Children's Cash Sales
PO Box 11
Falmouth
Cornwall
TR10 9EN

Please enclose a cheque or postal order or debit my Visa/ Access –

Credit card no:

Expiry date:

Signature:

– to the value of the cover price plus:

UK: 80p for the first book, and 20p per copy for each additional book ordered to a maximum charge of £2.00.

BFPO: 80p for the first book, and 20p per copy for each additional book.

Overseas and Eire: £1.50 for the first book, £1.00 for the second book, thereafter 30p per book.

Lions reserve the right to show new retail prices on covers which may differ from those previously advertised in the text or elsewhere.

Lions